MARYLAND SASQUATCH MASSACRE

ETHAN RICHARDS

MARYLAND SASQUATCH MASSACRE

WWW.SEVEREDPRESS.COM

ISBN: 978-1-923165-40-3

PROLOGUE:

Dahlia Rhodes shivered as she stepped into the dark. Her breath condensed in the crisp air of Savage River State Forest. She moved cautiously with her group of ten, maneuvering her heavy, black leather platform boot carefully over the barbed wire fence.

"Great," Dahlia muttered as the wire sliced through her pine-colored ski trousers. "Those weren't cheap."

A firm hand clamped down on her bicep, startling her. She spun around to face a golden-haired man with sapphire-colored eyes. His face was obscured by a black hoodie and a COVID-style face mask. The hoodie, though baggy, couldn't conceal his muscular build. An Anarchist "A" gleamed balefully on his chest, its crimson hue contrasting with the pallid moonlight.

"You gotta be quiet," the man whispered, his voice barely audible over the rustling leaves.

"O-okay, Dom," Dahlia stammered.

His grip tightened, and he leaned in closer. "And no names."

He released her and turned away, moving to the front of the group with a predator's grace. She watched him, her heart pounding against her ribs with a rapid, hummingbird-like rhythm. *Dominic Bennet*, she thought, *I'd follow you into hell.*

Her cheeks flushed, a mix of embarrassment from his scolding and the intensity of her crush on him. Despite her aversion to the patriarchy, Dominic was different. Dahlia knew why she gravitated toward movements like this—why she followed people like him. Since middle school, she'd been self-conscious about her vitiligo, the patches of pale skin that dotted her arms and face. It made her feel different. Lesser. It pushed her into the shadows of crowds who accepted outcasts, even if that meant embracing radical ideas.

She eased carefully over the barbed wire and adjusted the straps of her backpack, steeling herself for what lay ahead.

"Don't worry about him," her friend whispered. Her friend, dressed similarly to Dahlia, hid her dyed black hair under a rasta-style hat.

Dahlia wiped the hair away from her face, her self-consciousness evident. "What did you say, Vanessa?"

"Dom," Vanessa replied. "He's not the gentle professor right now; he's in full commando mode."

I can't believe I'm doing this, Dahlia thought.

Dahlia had participated in political protests before, but this was uncharted territory. She and Vanessa now followed a group of activists venturing through Savage River State Forest with a singular mission: vandalism. The Maryland State Government had controversially privatized this public land, selling it to Heinrich Aristov.

This type of environmental injustice ends with me, Dahlia vowed.

Despite her determination, a gnawing fear churned in her stomach. This was beyond the peaceful protests she once thought would be enough. But fear had never stopped her before—it was the shame of feeling invisible that had steered her down this path.

Aristov compounded his environmental crimes not only by robbing the working class of nature but also by neglecting his purchase. In his neglect, the bourgeoisie allowed the land to become a wild, untamed wilderness. As a child, Dahlia had roamed these woods, but now the paths were overgrown with thick, malevolent grass that clung to her feet like spectral tendrils.

"Alright, guys," Dominic called out, his voice slicing through the tension. "We're here."

Dahlia let down her backpack. Unzipping her pack, she pulled out her portable speaker. Then, taking an auxiliary cord, she plugged it into her smartphone.

"Wood-knocking," she said, scanning through the files on her phone.

She didn't understand the significance, but Dom stated that it was to show "establish dominance" and that it was "nature threatening humanity."

If he wasn't so hot, I'd make him explain more, she laughed.

The audio recording blasted through the speakers—*WHOOMP! WHOOMP! WHOOMP!*

The sound came so hard that Dahlia could feel the bass reverberate in her fingertips. The stereo made it hard to hear her friends. Looking up, she saw the others—the protestors acting similarly, pulling out their supplies—spray paint and cameras.

Then—among the chaos, she heard Vanessa's voice, "Dom?"

Her friend's voice had an almost childlike quality—Vanessa's confusion was evident in the tone.

"I just saw him...I saw him?" her friend cried.

"What do you mean?" Dahlia asked.

"He...he just left us—"

But her friend's voice fell mute. Dahlia was distracted by the paste that her friend had covered herself in.

"Vanessa?" Dahlia asked, "W-what is that?"

"Dom! Where are you?" Vanessa yelled.

Dahlia leaned forward. With a trembling hand, she touched the liquid that Vanessa had doused herself in.

"Is that...blood?" Dahlia asked.

"It's supposed to be a protest," Vanessa said, "Dom told me to do it. To say 'blood is on their hands.' But he—"

Dahlia touched the material. She brought it back to her nose and smelled it.

"Is that red food coloring?" Dahlia asked. "Is that—?"

Dahlia couldn't contain her curiosity and dapped her tongue with the material.

"Yep," Dahlia said, "that's honey...Dom had you douse yourself in honey?"

"Did you not hear anything I said?" Vanessa's words were rapid, and she breathed with short, shallow gasps, "I said he—"

WHOOMP! WHOOMP! WHOOMP!

Dahlia looked down at her speaker. It had been knocked over, with its face lying in the grass. The grass vibrated as the recording sounded.

She looked into the forest and realized these knocks were not coming from her speaker.

"That's coming from the trees," Vanessa said. "It's like—"

"They're knocking against them," Dahlia answered, "against the t—"

WHAAM!

Dahlia screamed as something fell into her. Shaking her head, she fought to see what was happening. Vanessa sagged against Dahlia.

"Vanessa?" Dahlia said as she braced against her friend.

Thump!

Vanessa's body slammed into the grass-covered soil.

Dahlia knelt beside her friend. She grabbed Vanessa's shoulder and shook it.

"This isn't funny," Dahlia said.

Vanessa made no response. Dahlia grunted and flipped her friend over. She touched her friend's face. She shivered as her fingers slipped into a cool liquid. Dahlia brought her finger to her face. She sniffed the material.

"Yuck," Dahlia said.

No, it wasn't the sweet aroma of honey - it was a distinctive metallic scent.

"Vanessa," she said and touched her friend's face.

There—on Vanessa's face, she felt a smooth stone. It was a softball-sized rock, almost a boulder. It had been buried hard into the scalp—with such force that it remained intact. Dahlia put her quaking fingers under Vanessa's nose—there was no breath.

"She's dead," Dahlia said.

But as she spoke, she felt a rush of wind, like something had jumped over her. She gagged as she felt a rush of wind consume her with an overwhelming odor. The scent, so terrible—caused the immediate release of tears and mucus.

A horrible human cry broke the night air. The shrill, fright-filled cry overpowered the audio recording. Another body—one of the men—flew through the air and slammed next to Vanessa's carcass. Instantly, she knew the man was dead.

Dahlia stood up and screamed. She sprinted. Lactic acid tore into her legs and chest as she moved.

Something pierced her leg. An overwhelming piercing pain pricked her shin.

Looking down, she saw it—silver-colored zig-zag teeth trapped her right leg. The teeth of the device were painted in Dahlia's blood, pinning her in place.

"A bear trap?" Dahlia said, in horrific recognition of what ensnared her.

She opened her mouth to cry, but she gurgled as vomitus rushed from her throat.

The smell had returned.

The overwhelming odor.

Tears and mucus flooded her eyes—hindering her vision.

But in the chaos, she still saw it.

She saw a shape.

A colossal frame—eight feet in height, with a pyramid-shaped dome atop its fur-covered body. In the dimness of the night and with her tear-filled eyes, she couldn't see everything, but she saw yellow, chimpanzee-like fangs.

She writhed in pain and grabbed the bear trap with both hands, trying to free herself.

The ground shook beneath her as the monstrous form continued forward.

She fell to her side and tore at the trap. And as she did, she saw the creature stepping forward.

It wasn't the clawed foot of a bear. No, she cried as she saw it. The monster walked on distinct, orangutan-like toes.

She closed her eyes as the monster stepped forward.

PART I

CHAPTER 1

Ebenezer "Eerie Eb" Edwards slammed the door to his podcast studio, frustration simmering in his eyes. He leaned against the door for a moment, letting out a deep sigh. The room, cluttered with evidence of his quirky podcasting life, seemed to close in on him. Posters of conspiracy theories and psychobilly bands stared down at him, a stark reminder of the world he desperately wanted to immerse himself in full-time.

Pushing off from the door, he crossed the room to a modest wardrobe. He opened it, revealing a neatly organized array of tactical attire. The contrast was immediate: tie-dye shirts and mismatched socks on one side, crisp, professional clothing on the other. With a sense of resignation, he undressed.

He slipped off his tie-dye shirt, revealing a muscular chest and arms, the product of years of rigorous military training. His physique was impressive, a stark contrast to the eccentric persona he projected on his podcast. As he removed the mismatched socks and replaced them with a matching pair of black, high-quality socks, he felt the transformation beginning.

Next, he put on a pair of professional-looking boots, lacing them with practiced precision. The sturdy, polished footwear completed the foundation of his transformation. He reached for a collared polo shirt—black, with a small, discrete logo on the chest. Though the shirt was professional, it couldn't contain his Herculean build, the fabric stretching over his broad shoulders and muscular arms.

He moved to a small mirror mounted on the wall, squeezing a dab of hair gel into his palm. With methodical movements, he styled his hair, the gel giving it a sleek, controlled look. The final touch was a pair of tactical sunglasses. He slid them on, their reflective lenses hiding the turmoil in his eyes.

Taking a step back, he surveyed himself in the mirror. Gone was the eccentric podcaster obsessed with the supernatural. In his place stood a professional soldier, every inch of him exuding competence and discipline. But beneath the surface, the two identities clashed, each vying for dominance.

The life he led as a soldier and then in private security was one of duty and discipline—something learned, but not his natural personality. His true self posed an eccentric and child-like curiosity that enabled him to explore the mysteries of the world. This other life—the professional field had helped him grow up as a man, but was a stark contrast to the chaotic creativity that fueled his passion for podcasting.

With one last look around the room, he left, the door closing softly behind him. As he walked down his bare hallway, his thoughts were a jumble of frustration and longing. The life he led as a soldier was one of duty and discipline, but the world of his podcast called to him, a siren song of mystery and escape from his loneliness.

He knew that deep down, his fascination with the supernatural and conspiracy theories was more than just a hobby. It was a refuge, a place where he could lose himself and forget the isolation he felt. But for now, duty called, and Eerie Eb had to leave his dorky, passionate self behind and become the professional, muscular security contractor the world now saw.

As he walked out into the bright light of the day, the tactical sunglasses shielded his eyes from the solar rays, but couldn't do the same for the frustration that tormented his soul.

CHAPTER 2

Eb moved swiftly through the narrow corridors of his apartment building. He kept his head down, avoiding eye contact. People were nothing but distractions—interruptions to the quiet space where his ideas thrived. Rather than suffer the small talk and awkward silences of the elevator, he took the stairs.

He pressed against the stairwell's exit door, the heavy click breaking the silence. The sudden brightness outside was almost offensive, the sun an overbearing reminder of everything he tried to avoid. Squinting against the harsh light, he scanned the parking lot, already irritated by the thought of returning to the world where expectations and obligations loomed.

"There you are," Eb muttered when he finally spotted his vehicle.

The black Suzuki Sidekick stood out, not because of its make but because it looked like a relic from another life—his life. The vehicle had been customized, lifted high with oversized, mud-caked tires, a far cry from the typical city car. It was a fortress on wheels, designed for the kind of isolation he craved. The deep tire treads were more at home in the swamps of Blackwater National Wildlife Refuge than in the confines of the paved parking lot.

He ran his hand over the scratched-up door, feeling a rare connection to the machine. It didn't need conversation, didn't judge him or expect anything. It just existed, ready to escape at a moment's notice.

"Back to the salt mines," he grumbled to himself, sliding into the driver's seat.

Before pulling out, he plugged in his smartphone, connecting it to the aftermarket radio he had installed years ago. The technology in the old Sidekick was just as much of a misfit as he was—an oddball contraption that only he could truly appreciate.

With a quick glance left and right, he set his phone to one of his latest podcast episodes. The sound of his own voice poured through the speakers.

"Yes," Eb muttered, settling into the familiar hum of his words, "I do like to listen to myself talk."

The episode roared to life, filling the silence as he drove off, leaving the parking lot and all its unwelcome humanity in the rearview mirror.

***

Eerie Ebenezer Podcast – Special Guest Elias Arian, Author of Born Among the Stars: The Case for Humanity's Extraterrestrial Past

Eerie Ebenezer *(laughing)*: *Alright, folks, welcome back to the Eerie Ebenezer Podcast, where we dig into the mysteries of life, the universe, and that thing your neighbor swears he saw in the woods. Today, we've got something extra special—joining us all the way from Wales is Elias Arian, author of the mind-bending book* Born Among the Stars: The Case for Humanity's Extraterrestrial Past. *Elias, man, thanks for being here.*

Elias Arian: *Diolch yn fawr, Eb. Glad to be on the show. Let's see what trouble we can stir up, eh?*

Eerie Eb: *Same here, dude. Now, I've been dying to talk about this. Your book – and correct me if I'm wrong – pretty much says that humans didn't evolve on Earth. We're not from here, and that's why we've got sunburns, back pain, all that jazz. You're saying we're cosmic convicts, exiled here as punishment, right?*

Elias Arian *(chuckling)*: *Well, that's one way to sum it up. The hypothesis I present suggests that* Homo sapiens *possess a number of biological traits that don't quite sync up with Earth's ecosystem. Our vulnerability to ultraviolet radiation, our spinal issues, and even our circadian misalignment with the planet's natural cycles all point toward an extraterrestrial origin. Earth might've been the penal colony, so to speak.*

Eerie Eb: *Right, so cosmic convicts. I gotta admit, that theory slaps. But here's my take—humans, we're just animals. Plain and simple. We're out here just trying to survive. Like, take Sasquatch—now that's a dude I can get behind. He's not worried about social standing or climbing some corporate ladder. He's just out in the woods, doing his thing, staying alive. That's us too, at the core—animals.*

Elias Arian *(laughing)*: *Aye, you're barking up the wrong tree with that one, Eb. Sounds like a typical childless bachelor talking to me! You haven't had the joy of being woken up at 3 AM by a teething infant, have you?*

Eerie Eb *(laughing)*: *Do I really have a member of the scientific community calling me a misanthrope? C'mon, man!*

Elias Arian *(teasing)*: *Well, if the* esgid *fits, mate—wear it! In Wales, we've got a saying, 'Yn anad dim, dyn ydy dyn'—'Above all, a man is still a man.' But you're taking too simplistic a view. Yes, we've got base instincts, but humans aren't just animals. Our neuroplasticity, abstract thinking, and complex social structures put us in a different category.*

Eerie Eb: *Alright, alright. But seriously, you think humans are more than just animals?*

Elias Arian: *Let's not go* cwtsio bant *now. Biologically, we are animals—mammals, even. But that doesn't tell the whole story. Look at our higher cognitive functions, our moral reasoning, and our capacity for empathy. These are things that set us apart. Even if you subscribe to the idea of us being cosmic exiles, as I suggest in the book, it's not just black and white.*

Eerie Eb: *I don't know, man. I still think we're just animals dressing it up with social rules.*

Elias Arian: *I get that. But even animals have codes, Eb. Maybe we're not perfect, maybe we're exiled troublemakers, but that doesn't take away the fact that human life is sacred. We just sometimes forget what that means. There's something more—human life transcends basic animal behavior.*

CHAPTER 3

Eb sighed as he parked his customized Suzuki Sidekick in the parking lot. Grimacing, he stared at his employer's office building. It was a Connex building with air-conditioning units crudely attached to makeshift windows. Though almost humorous in its design, the building was strategic. It circumvented zoning laws, and—in the event the unit deployed—all equipment could be thrown into the Connex, strapped down, and shipped.

"Yo, yo, yo," a voice called out, "it's Eerie Ebenezer!"

So it starts, Eb sighed.

A Caucasian man with bleached blonde hair and a precision-trimmed, ruddy chin-curtain beard stepped out from his glistening, black-coated Chevrolet Impala. The man possessed a physique worthy of bodybuilding competitions at the professional level. As he walked forward, he removed hip-hop-inspired diamond-studded earrings from each ear. The Herculean figure had a tattoo sleeve visible from his right bicep that extended to his wrist.

Johnny Chapel, Eb thought. *AKA Dirty Chap the Wankster.*

"Dawg," Dirty Chap said, "If I had to guess you drove a rock-crawler, that jeeplet is 'zactly the whip I'd picture you drivin'."

"I figured you'd like it," Eb sneered, "it's something straight out of a Funky Bunch video."

"Ah-ha!" Dirty Chap laughed, covering his mouth with a closed fist. He stepped forward, offering Eb a fist pound.

Grimacing, Eb accepted.

"I appreciate the Marky Mark reference..."

"You mean," Eb narrowed his eyes, studying Dirty Chap, "the actor Mark Wahlberg?"

"Yeah," Dirty Chap said, "that's what I said."

How did this guy survive in the Marine Corps? Eb thought.

But the reality was that Eb knew. Though enigmatic in his speech and appearance, Dirty Chap was a beast. He possessed twenty-two-inch biceps—the same mass as Arnold Schwarzenegger during the golden era. In addition to his physical prowess, Dirty Chap was an excellent marksman and possessed a great tactical mind. Though peculiar, his voice sang out smooth on the radio, keeping a tense situation calm.

"I like you, man," Dirty Chap said to Eb. "You're a character. You're active, resourceful, always pushin' forward but dang, dawg, you are weird!"

Eb gritted his teeth. Eb wasn't stupid—he was self-aware. He had served in the military since he was seventeen years old and had just left the service, dabbled in law enforcement, and now worked as a Security Contractor.

The truth was he loved the job but never fit in. He had sat through horrible peer evaluations and Field Training Officers who had tried to convince him he had Asperger's syndrome. He had been able to manage in the past, but in recent years, Eb had evolved into what some of his friends had described as a "grouchy old man."

"How's that podcast goin'?" Dirty Chap asked.

In the previous encounters, Eb would have warmed up to the invitation to divulge his latest endeavors into paranormal research. Still, his irritation at his return to the "real world" made it feel impossible.

"I'm getting close," Eb said. "Getting so close to doing that type of stuff full-time. The paycheck from this should hopefully set that up."

Dirty Chap's eyes lit up. "For reals?"

Eb nodded.

"Congrats, man. You're almost there."

Yes, Eb thought, *almost.*

Almost out of the lifestyle he had grown to hate. He was twenty-seven now—ten years of misery. Almost free from the professional field that had hazed and bullied him since he was seventeen years old.

"Do you know anything about this assignment?" Eb asked.

"Not specifics," Dirty Chap said, "but word on the street is, it's local."

"As in here in the DC Metropolitan area?" Eb asked.

"Nah, dawg," Dirty Chap said. "Local as in Maryland. I heard we're out in the sticks."

"No joke?" Eb scratched his head.

Their focus was mainly on securing individuals and routes, while other crews were selected for more exotic locations.

"Yeah," Dirty Chap said. "Too bad it's your last, I heard this is a call to the Big Leagues."

Eb pretended to appear frustrated. The reality was that in this profession, Eb just wanted a paycheck. He had no desire to be—as Dirty Chap had described it—a "top dawg, triggah pullah."

I don't want to 'do my best,' Eb thought. *I want to give a comfortable 60% and have time for my podcast.*

Giving a 100% effort hurt. While on Active Duty, Eb had leaders who would get to work at 0400 and leave at 2300 hours, and then the subordinates felt pressured to stay late, too. How could you compete against that?

The answer was even less sleep and more time spent at work. Eb's quirky personality had prevented him from feeling like he was ever "one of the guys," and the long hours required kept him in that environment.

"So we're heading to the woods," Eb said, "where to?"

"Out west, to Garrett County," Dirty Chap said. "To Savage River State Forest."

CHAPTER 4

Eerie Eb and Dirty Chap walked into the customized Connex. The air was heavy with the scent of metal accompanied by the faint hum of a generator in the background. The space was filled with a blend of high-tech equipment and old-school military pragmatism, every item meticulously placed, every detail screaming efficiency and readiness.

"Wassup?" Dirty Chap said as he entered the room, his voice cutting through the quiet with the grace of a mallet.

Seven men, all dressed in similar professional attire, turned their attention to the newcomers. Dirty Chap, with his usual unrestrained enthusiasm, greeted each team member, his energy contagious. Eb, still wrestling with his recent plunge back into reality, begrudgingly offered a fist pound to each.

A dry-erase board hung on the wall, displaying a detailed topographical map of the Savage River State Forest. As Eb and Dirty Chap approached the board, a tall, muscular black man stepped forward. He handed them a binder, his movements precise and deliberate.

"Thanks, boss," Dirty Chap said, taking the binder with a nod.

Eb greeted the man similarly, accepting the binder. Jacques Greenwood, their leader, exemplified military bearing and leadership. Eb would have admired Jacques' style if he weren't so disgruntled by their current situation.

Jacques Greenwood had been a Division II All-American Defensive End for the Bowie State University Bulldogs. During his time there, he participated in the Coast Guard's College Student Pre-Commissioning Initiative, later serving as an Ensign in a Port Security Unit. *This guy knows his stuff,* Eb thought.

"Ol' Appalachia and the Muleskinner did us a solid with this product," Dirty Chap said, pointing at the binder with evident appreciation.

"Yes, they did," Jacques replied, his voice calm and authoritative.

Ol' Appalachia, Eb thought, glancing at the man. Dirty Chap referred to Casper "Appalachia" Cresap, a native of Allegany County, Maryland. His red hair, cauliflower ears, and hipster-style glasses made Appalachia's appearance distinct.

Casper had served in Naval Intelligence and then in Customs and Border Protection in the Office of Field Operations before being selected for the Special Response Team. Once he discovered the lucrative nature of private security, he resigned and joined this unit.

"Dawg's already got the terrain analysis knocked out," Dirty Chap said, his excitement evident.

Eb rolled his eyes at Dirty Chap's use of the word "dawg." But Dirty Chap was correct; a transparent sheet hung over the map, decorated with precise marks showing potential routes and natural obstacles in the area.

"Impressive," Eb said, observing the level of professionalism presented in the binder.

"Muleskinner helped me out," Appalachia said, nodding towards Valjean "Muleskinner" Pinkney.

Dirty Chap greeted the wiry black man with a handshake. Muleskinner had worked as a Postal police officer and a Quartermaster in the Marine Corps Reserve before joining the team. His combination of security and logistics expertise enabled him to procure the right equipment at the right time.

Muleskinner nodded in acknowledgment, a hint of embarrassment flickering in his eyes.

"Hey, there's the Seabee!" Dirty Chap greeted another man with a firm handshake.

Accidental, Eb thought, *our demolitions expert.*

Sawyer "Accidental" Burroughs hadn't seen much action in terms of offensive operations due to the nature of their missions. Accidental had served as a Seabee in the US Navy. His nickname stemmed from his residence in the tiny town of Accident, Maryland, combined with a bit of dark humor regarding the explosives expert's lack of precision.

Eb eyed the last two members of the team.

Ercole Bonaparte, simply "Doc," was the team's medic. A Paramedic and Firefighter out of Bethesda, Doc's unusual schedule allowed him to work full-time with the unit. Eb watched as Doc traced his fingers over the map, highlighting items in his binder with meticulous care.

And there's the shyster, Eb thought.

The final member of the team was legal expert Marcus Mattucks. Marcus had served in the Air Force Security Forces before earning his undergraduate and Juris Doctor degrees from the University of Baltimore.

Eb scratched his head as he studied the binder.

"We've never done anything like this before," Eb said, looking over at Marcus. "Are we up for this?"

"Like I said," Dirty Chap replied, "we're moving up."

That's strange, Eb thought. *Personnel recovery?*

"How did we get this?" Eb asked, his curiosity piqued.

"You can ask her," Jacques said, pointing with his chin.

Eb turned, looking in the direction Jacques had indicated.

There, sitting quietly in the corner, was a woman. She had jet-black hair and wore cargo pants and a utility-style shirt. Her skin displayed a piebald pattern from apparent vitiligo, making it impossible to determine her ethnicity.

"Who is that?" Dirty Chap asked, his voice rising with each syllable.

Eb nudged Dirty Chap in the ribs, encouraging him to lower his voice.

"That's her, gentlemen," Jacques said. "This is our client."

Eb, along with the others on his team, sat behind the desk. He studied the binder in his hand, looking up as Jacques and the woman spoke.

"This is Cora Rhodes," Jacques said, pointing at the seated woman with his binder.

"That's your sister?" Dirty Chap asked, his finger stabbing at the binder like it was a guilty party.

Cora nodded.

"And she started running with these hippies?" Dirty Chap asked, his voice dripping with incredulity. Eb dug his tongue into his bottom lip, feeling a rising tide of frustration with Dirty Chap's interruptions.

"Hippies doesn't accurately describe it," Jacques said. "When I think of hippies, I think of Woodstock. These guys..."

"Are, at times," Cora said, interjecting, "a bit more radical...mostly tranquil, but sometimes a little off."

No, Princess, Eb thought, reading through the information. *Your sister and these guys are domestic terrorists.*

Eb's mind rushed to the names his paranormal friends had been called. On more than one occasion, his groups and their isolationist cohorts had been called white supremacists, with academics branding them with even worse labels

And this rich girl was literally running around with Molotov cocktails and marketed as just "a little off."

"This doesn't even make sense," Eb said, shaking his head. "Burning SUVs to protest the environment? How many pollutants does that release?"

Eb looked up. The woman's face was a storm of embarrassment, pain, and finally, a flash of anger as she locked eyes with Eb.

"Buddy," a voice hissed from the shadows, and turning, he saw Dirty Chap pressing a finger to his lips, urging Eb to hold his tongue.

Oh, come on, Eb thought, feeling the weight of Dirty Chap's silent reprimand.

"She's still," Cora said, her voice hard, "my sister."

Rich kids and their politics, Eb thought, his eyes narrowing as he studied Cora. She looked to be in her mid-twenties; the report said Dahlia was younger. Images flickered through his mind Jane Fonda posing with a North Vietnamese anti-aircraft gun, the wealthy attorney in his hometown who started as a hard-nosed DA but now had a daughter calling for the defunding of police

And now this brat is putting us all in jeopardy, Eb thought, feeling a sneer curl his lips. Despite his financial needs, he stared back at her, letting her see the full measure of his disdain.

He knew she knew why he hated her. He had been stuck living paycheck to paycheck, and now he was forced to take orders from this heiress. His anger simmered, barely contained. In his adult life, he had been pushed around so much that his ability to restrain his irritation had worn thin.

Toxic leaders and jealous coworkers—Eb had put up with them all his adult life because he needed the work. Bosses and instructors had picked up on his quirks and made him a target, but he had to endure it because he needed the money.

But this heiress never did, Eb thought. In her self-professed open-mindedness and tolerance, he was sure she was more judgmental than any evangelical.

Could you imagine the hell she'd raise if a barista got her order wrong? Eb thought.

Eb closed his eyes, trying to focus away from the growing frustration. He had struck paranormal gold—the rush of research, the podcasts, the networking, and the relentless push forward; now he was earning money. He'd finally found a field where people respected him. And this new pursuit had gotten him out in the woods, away from people. Eb smiled. He opened his eyes, and there, sitting before him, was Cora—the heiress with raven-colored hair pulled back very tightly and vitiligo-painted skin—staring back at him.

"Falling asleep during a brief, Eb?" she asked.

With involuntary reflexes, Eb felt his hands ball into fists.

"Just...adjusting my focus," he said, his voice tight. "Do you have a problem with me?"

He felt immediate regret at his words. He needed this job. Sure, he hated her, and she hated him back, but the paycheck forced his hand.

"Eb," Jacques called out.

Heat rushed through Eb's body. Beads of sweat balled on his head. He was embarrassed—publicly. First by Dirty Chap, then by the brat, and now by his boss.

I can't take this crap anymore, Eb thought, feeling adrenaline surge through his body. His hands began to shake. He wanted to throw his binder to the ground, stand up and direct two extended middle fingers at this black-haired battle axe.

With his remaining self-restraint, he fought to contain his hate.

You need this, Eb thought to himself.

He cast a hate-filled gaze at his boss and then initiated vinyasa-style breathing—sucking in air for six seconds, holding it for four, and releasing it for four. The intense pulse in his throat began to fade. Finally, he nodded.

"I apologize for any distraction, ma'am," Eb said, forcing the words out.

Cora's eyes locked onto his. Eb forced a subservient expression, lowering his gaze, allowing her to believe she had triumphed.

Eb liked Sasquatch because it was simple. The Sasquatch and the Homo sapien were both apes; they were both animals. But Sasquatch, unlike his human cousins, didn't play these silly games. Sasquatch didn't care if you polished your boots before the duty day. Sasquatch didn't care if you forgot to shave before shift.

But people did. And these silly games had kept Eb from ever feeling like he fit in. Eb had actually been gifted as a tactician and fighter. He could survive in nature, but these politics, these weird games humans played, had made him a pariah. He didn't have the social polish to know when to speak and when to be quiet. He would willingly spend hours cleaning his Glock, but refused to expend energy on polishing boots. He hated these charades. And right now, this farce meant that Cora Rhodes was his boss.

He'd play the part. He'd work for Cora Rhodes, but there would be no passion. He'd put no additional effort into this mission because the reality was, he really didn't care if some spoiled rich girl had vanished.

The Baltimore Inquirer

Conservative and Liberal Protesters Unite Against Privatization of Savage River State Forest

Garrett County, MD – A tale of dark deals and unlikely alliances unfolds in the Old Line State. Conservative and liberal protesters have converged on Savage River State Forest Park, a sprawling 54,000-acre haven now threatened by a shadowy sale to Heinrich Aristov, the enigmatic CEO with a reputation as murky as a back-alley noir.

A Common Cause: Protecting Nature and Local Interests

For the liberals, it's a classic narrative of capitalist greed devouring sanctity. "This is yet another instance of the working class being crushed by corporate interests," spat Rebecca Rodney, an environmental firebrand. "Turning it over to this capitalist pig takes advantage of the very communities it was intended to benefit."

On the conservative side, the sentiment is equally venomous.

"This isn't true capitalism," snarled Harold Heshmire a local business owner and head of the conservative protest group., "this sale reeks of corruption. Heinrich Aristov represents a brand of corporate elitism that masquerades as progressive but is anything but. This deal will strangle real estate opportunities, drive costs, and ultimately choke the local economy."

A Controversial Figure

Heinrich Aristov. The name slithers through the shadows like a snake. Known for his polarizing stances and veiled motives, Aristov's plan to transform parts of the forest into a series of eco-friendly resorts and exclusive retreats has been met with skepticism and outright hostility.

"Aristov's so-called eco-friendly resorts are a smokescreen," hissed Dr. Daniel Marx, a biologist with a nose for the sordid truth. "His track record shows a pattern of

prioritizing profit over genuine environmental stewardship. The privatization of Savage River State Forest is not about conservation; it's about creating a playground for the wealthy at the expense of the public."

United in Purpose

Despite their clashing ideologies, conservatives and liberals have found common ground in their fight against Aristov's creeping influence. Joint rallies, community meetings, and coordinated social media campaigns have formed a robust and vocal opposition that transcends traditional political divides.

"What's happening here is unprecedented," said key protest organizer Jesse Perot. "We're seeing people who would normally be at each other's throats come together because they recognize a shared threat. This isn't about left or right; it's about protecting our heritage and ensuring that our natural resources remain in public hands."

The Road Ahead

As the battle drags on, both sides brace for a grueling fight. Legal challenges, public hearings, and relentless on-the-ground activism are set to define the coming months. The state government, caught in the crossfire, faces mounting pressure to reconsider the sale and explore alternative means of managing the forest that does not involve privatization.

For now, Savage River State Forest stands as a symbol of unity amidst chaos, a testament to the power of shared purpose in preserving what truly matters. A story of greed, resistance, and improbable alliances unfolds in the shadows of those ancient trees. Whether this united front can ultimately thwart the privatization efforts remains to be seen, but one thing is clear: the fight for Savage River State Forest has only just begun.

CHAPTER 5

Inside the Connex, Eb sat at the desk. With meticulous fingers he loaded rounds into his magazines.

"She's a beauty," he murmured to himself. With tender fingers he patted the disassembled Desert Tech MDR. His passions had shifted from the intricate dance of tactics, yet certain elements drew him back with an irresistible pull—the evocative scent of CLP, the comforting feel of a carbine snugly synched with a customized sling, and the rhythmic exertion of a patrol hike. The Desert Tech MDR revived his spirit, a self-loading bullpup carbine that made his heart beat faster.

"Hey, Eb!" a voice called out.

Eb shook his head and with reluctance pulled his eyes away from his task. Turning to the door, he saw Jacques standing there, hands on his hips. Eb's stomach tightened. Jacques beckoned him over, and Eb nodded, rising to his feet with a quick, purposeful stride.

What is this about? Eb wondered.

He placed his loose ammunition and magazines on the table, then walked toward Jacques with determined steps.

"What's up?" Eb asked, his voice calm, though his mind buzzed with questions.

Jacques waved him further away from the door.

"You tell me, man," he said, crossing his arms over his chest.

"I was talking with the woman," Eb replied, his eyes wandering, searching for Cora. In the corner of his eye, he spied her seated in a sleek Mercedes-Benz S-Class, her phone pressed to her ear, engaged in apparent earnest conversation.

"That's an S-Klasse," Jacques noted, a hint of admiration coloring his voice.

Eb sighed.

"C'mon, Eb," Jacques continued. "This is our organization's next step. She's got a brand-new vehicle, she's connected, and she specifically asked for us."

Despite himself, Eb glanced back at Cora, then returned his gaze to Jacques.

"She did?" he asked, scratching his head.

"Yes," Jacques affirmed. "And I love you, Eb, but I tried to shelf you for this mission. You looked like you wanted to kill her."

"What?" Eb felt a surge of adrenaline course through his veins, his eyes narrowing.

"But I didn't," Jacques quickly added.

"Thanks," Eb said, his shoulders slumping as he sighed, eyes cast downward.

I have no control, he thought.

"Don't thank me," Jacques said. "As the leader, I also have to market Dark Waters to the customer. I told her I was getting rid of you, but she stopped me."

Eb felt his face twist into a complex mask of anger and confusion.

"No loyalty, huh?" Eb asked.

"Don't test me, Eb," Jacques warned. "You know it's nothing personal. You're a good guy—"

"But," Eb interrupted, "I'm a 'but guy.' 'He's good, but...'" Eb's hands clenched into fists, his voice rising in volume.

"You gotta calm down," Jacques said. "You know it's not like that with me. Yes, you're eccentric, but I always tried to look out for you, and you looked like you wanted to hurt that lady."

Eb's stomach dropped.

"I never wanted that," he said. "I'm...tired—"

"We're all tired," Jacques replied. "I can't justify the way you treated a client. But she said she wanted *you.* She told me not to shelf you."

"That makes no sense," Eb said.

"She must have done her research," Jacques explained. "She specifically chose this team. There were others, but she found us and picked us. She said you were too skilled to let go."

Eb opened his mouth, about to ask another question, but stopped. He scratched his head. "Really?"

"Like I said," Jacques pointed toward Cora with his chin, "she's done her research."

Eb looked back again. Cora still sat in the driver's seat but was now working on her cell phone. She wasn't mindlessly scrolling but typing away with her thumbs, treating her phone not as a social media extension but as a tool for communication.

"You know she basically lost her sister, right?" Jacques asked. "If we can recover her, she's probably going to face at least some sort of legal liability."

"Her sister's a rich kid," Eb snorted. "She'll survive."

"Survive?" Jacques gasped. "Eb, we really don't know if she's *alive.* That's 54,000 acres of wilderness; she's out there with thugs calling themselves activists. That girl is probably dead and I think Cora knows it. And you're glaring at her the week after her little sister disappeared."

A cloud of guilt hung over Eb.

"I haven't known you that long," Jacques said, "but I can see you've changed."

"What do you mean?" Eb asked.

"You used to be pleasant. You'd crack jokes, almost like a humorous chaplain," Jacques said. "It created a good atmosphere."

"Like I said I'm tired—"

"Tired of what?" Jacques threw both hands up in apparent exasperation. "Tired of people?"

Eb nodded.

"Well," Jacques shook his head. "Even if you do get to work full-time in your unusual field, you're still going to be dealing with people. I can't help you there."

Jacques shook his head and walked back inside, leaving Eb alone. Looking down at the ground, he kicked at a pebble.

Anger consumed Eb. Not because Jacques was wrong. No. He was frustrated because Jacques was right.

The Baltimore Inquirer

What is Heinrich Aristov Hiding?

Garrett County, MD – The picturesque expanse of Savage River State Forest, known for its natural beauty and wildlife, may be hiding more than meets the eye. In a shocking twist, workers involved in a mysterious project along the Savage River have blown the whistle on Heinrich Aristov, the elusive CEO with a reputation for secrecy and shadowy deals. What started as a conservation effort has now raised more questions than answers.

Strange Projects and Ominous Outcomes

According to insiders, workers have been tasked with constructing artificial rock habitats – known as "mock rock" – all along the river. These constructions, allegedly intended as habitats for black bears, are raising red flags across the environmental and political spectrum. "It all seems friendly on the surface," one worker revealed under anonymity. "But the truth is, no one knows the end game here. Why black bears? Why now? It's all a little too convenient."

What appears to be a wildlife project could have darker implications. Ecologists are now sounding the alarm, comparing the potential outcome to Florida's disastrous Python invasion, where a once-contained species devastated local ecosystems. "We're playing with fire here," warned Dr. Karen Helmsley, an ecologist tracking wildlife patterns in the area. "An increased black bear population could have serious, irreversible consequences. This isn't conservation – this is exploitation."

The Pika Controversy

As if the black bear project weren't enough, rumors have surfaced that Aristov's plans might involve releasing non-

native species, such as the pika, into the forest. Animal rights organizations are furious. "This would be an ecological disaster in the making," stated Randall Pierce, president of the Wildlife Rescue Coalition. "Introducing an animal like the pika into a non-native environment is reckless and shows a complete disregard for natural balance. Aristov is playing god with our ecosystem."

Smoke and Mirrors or Sinister Plans?

All of this begs the question: What exactly is Heinrich Aristov hiding? Is his eco-friendly narrative a cover for something more nefarious? Or is this just the latest example of a corporate mogul manipulating nature for profit?

Critics from both sides of the aisle are speaking out. "This reeks of corruption," remarked Harold Heshmire, a local business owner. "Heinrich Aristov is not the savior he pretends to be. This isn't about preserving nature – it's about controlling it."

Meanwhile, environmentalists see it as a classic case of corporate greed. "He's taking something that belongs to the public and twisting it to suit his bottom line," said Rebecca Rodney, an environmental activist. "It's the Everglades all over again."

The Fight for Transparency

As both conservatives and liberals unite in protest, the pressure mounts for Aristov to come clean. Joint rallies, legal actions, and community meetings have emerged as a formidable opposition. Local officials have called for investigations into the project, and public hearings are now being scheduled.

So, what is Heinrich Aristov really up to in Savage River State Forest? Only time will tell, but one thing is clear: The fight for the truth is just beginning.

CHAPTER 6

Eb grunted as he climbed into the vehicle. In addition to his podcast and research, he displayed discipline in staying in decent shape. But despite his fitness, it still required effort to get into the vehicle.

With a shrewdness befitting a military quartermaster, Muleskinner had found funds to purchase an Avtoros Shaman. The enigmatic six-wheeled vehicle was perfect for personnel protection, and its rugged design would be ideal for their trek into the Savage River Forest.

"You know, Muleskinner," Dirty Chap said as he buckled his seatbelt, "I always heard that you supply guys were the most "honest, dishonest" cats around."

"'Most honest dishonest," Muleskinner's laughter filled the vehicle. "I think that explains some supply guy perceptions. Jacques had quite the reaction when I told him about our purchase. He said, 'Thank you, but I don't want to know.'" The team burst into laughter, their surprise and appreciation evident.

The team laughed. Eb remained silent, not speaking to the others, but stowed his carbine in the vertical gun rack beside his seat with focused effort and his assault pack in the seat below.

"Although," Dirty Chap said, "I've gotta say, I'm just as impressed with Marcus for gettin' this thing street legal."

Eb looked around the group, remembering Jacques' admonishment and attempted humor: "If you think supply sergeants are honest, dishonest guys, what does that make a good lawyer?"

But the others didn't laugh and, with sullen eyes, looked at Eb. Eb winced. With complete apathy to his coworkers' response, Eb angrily threw up his hands and refocused on his assault pack. He pulled out the radio and began working the settings to his personal preference. Next, he pulled out his tactical laptop and worked with it.

Eb shifted his eyes from left to right, looking through the team. He had been deliberate in sitting in the back of the vehicle, not just so that he could have room to work on his setup and to give himself space from others, but also because he wanted to work on his podcast. He needed to send emails, correspond with others in the field, and search for guests.

He was technically using his personal computer to work, but he was using the company's Wi-Fi to complete personal correspondence. He turned on the company's tactical hotspot and started to work. The smartwatch on his wrist dinged, and he read the screen.

"Hey," Eb called to the driver, "are you getting this?"

At the front, in the center-seated driver location, Appalachia slightly turned his head, acknowledging Eb's call.

"What's up?" Appalachia asked.

"This is saying we're going to have a two-hour delay going this way," Eb said, pointing at his smartwatch.

"Yeah," Appalachia called back, "there's quite a bit of traffic up ahead."

Eb scratched his head. Typically, traffic went east and north, but it could sometimes be sparse on the path to western Maryland.

"I'm kind of embarrassed," Appalachia said. "I picked the route, I studied the geography of the forest, but I didn't see any events that would have caused this big of a delay."

"Don't beat yourself up," Eb said. "How could you know what's happening in every little town between here and Garrett County?"

"I still got family out here," Appalachia said. "There should have been some gossip, something that would have let me know."

"Yeah," Eb said, "but you're busy. You can't keep up with your family; you've got a job. You're busy—"

"They're my family," Appalachia said, cutting him off. "They're *my* people."

Eb felt his face flushing red again. *People.* This made the second time he'd been preached to about the importance of people.

"I'm just saying, you can't know everything, Appalachia," Eb said. "I'm not a people pleaser, so you know if I'm saying you're okay, then you're okay. Plus, Virginia has some pretty aggressive traffic laws. Maybe people are just trying to avoid that."

"No," Appalachia called out, "I think I see what it is."

"What do you mean?" Eb asked.

"I mean, I think I see what's clogging up the road," Appalachia said.

"Oh yeah?"

"I think..." Appalachia started, "I think it's some kind of procession. I think it's a funeral."

Why Are So Many People in Maryland Dying from Snake Bites?

In a startling trend, five people in Maryland have died from snake bites this year alone. This is an alarming deviation from the national average, where approximately 7,000–8,000 people are bitten by venomous snakes annually in the United States, but only about five fatalities occur nationwide. The sudden spike in deaths has left authorities scrambling for answers.

Who Gets Bitten?

Contrary to what one might expect, these fatalities did not occur in remote rural areas. Instead, the deaths were reported in Cumberland and Hagerstown. "I've never seen anything like it," said Dr. Kishore of Frostburg State University. "These types of fatalities were more common in my home country, so I am shocked to see them here."

What's Changed?

Experts are investigating significant ecological and behavioral changes in the Eastern Copperhead and the Timber Rattlesnake species. Dr. Kishore noted, "There seems to be not just an ecological change but also a behavioral shift in these snakes."

In an intriguing twist, Dr. Kishore mentioned reports from colleagues in South Dakota about Prairie Rattlesnakes with atrophied tail muscles. "There is a debate whether this is a result of unnatural selection—where louder rattlesnakes are being killed—or if we are witnessing a new stage of evolution," he explained.

Typically found in the forested areas of Garrett County, these snakes appear to be experiencing displacement. "This is particularly interesting because there hasn't been an increase in human activity in the area," said Dr. Kishore. When asked to clarify "displacement," he explained, "In layman's terms—something's pushing these creatures out."

Authorities and researchers are now racing to understand the causes behind this unusual pattern and to implement measures to prevent further tragedies.

CHAPTER 7

"Snake bites?" Eb asked, peering over the document. He lifted his gaze from the screen, eyes scanning the room, searching for Ercole "Doc" Bonaparte. "Yo, Doc!"

Doc emerged from his thoughts, his face twisted in a sneer that curled his lip in an involuntary manner. Eb felt an icy chill of self-consciousness creep over him, a dread that gnawed at the edges of his composure.

"You got antivenom?" Eb asked, his face flushing deeper with each word.

Doc's sneer sharpened, but his eyes gleamed with apparent curiosity. "Antivenom? For what?"

Eb pointed a trembling finger at his laptop. "There's been an uptick in rattlesnakes and copperheads in this area."

Doc frowned, a deep line creasing his forehead. "That doesn't make a lick of sense. Snakes avoid people."

"Snakes *here* do," Eb said, his voice quieter now, almost a whisper.

Doc's eyes bore into him. "What do you mean?"

"Snakes in North America, sure," Eb said, his voice gaining strength, "but elsewhere—Southeast Asia, Africa—not so much."

"That's not true," Doc said, a hint of impatience in his voice. "I don't know what kind of crazy, otherworldly nonsense you've been reading—"

"It's the same reason people in Africa don't swim in the rivers," Eb said, his voice rising. "People don't own it."

"What are you saying, Eerie?" Doc asked.

"I'm saying there's a lot of nasty stuff out the African bush," Eb said, his words tumbling out in a rush.

"In Africa?" Doc asked, his tone skeptical, almost mocking.

Eb shook his head in a quick, vehement motion. "I know what you're implying—that because I'm into conspiracies, I'm some kind of white supremacist saying Africa is a wasteland. But that ain't it—that ain't it at all, Doc. African flora and fauna are just different. We have alligators—they have crocodiles. We have bison—they have elephants. We have coral snakes—they have cobras. They can't swim in creeks or lakes because they don't know what's there. Why should a cobra fear man when it has to contend with hippos?"

"And all of that," Doc said, his voice heavy with sarcasm, "all that random information, how does that tie into us? Into us right here?"

Eb sighed, a deep, weary sound, closing his eyes to focus, to steady himself against the torrent of frustration. "It's simple."

"Snakes are going into metropolitan areas," Doc said, the skepticism thick in his voice. "That doesn't seem simple at all—"

"You're a man of medicine, right?" Eb asked, his voice sharp. "Doesn't bacteria resist antibiotics?"

"Not the same—"

"Exactly the same," Eb insisted, his voice fierce, determined. "It's the concept, not the specifics."

"So, you're saying snakes are going into Hagerstown," Doc laughed, a harsh, incredulous sound, "because bacteria resist antibiotics? What's wrong with you?"

"No," Eb said, his voice unyielding. "I'm talking about the principle. The bacteria fight back and ultimately...they...it...however you classify bacteria...no longer has to worry about antibiotics. It can move without fear of any retaliation."

"That's not exactly how bacteria works," Doc said.

"Bacteria—man—monkeys," Eb said, "it's *all* the same...just different ladders on the rung of evolution."

"Ah," Doc said, smiling, "I see where you're trying to paint a picture. So, Eerie Ebenezer, what are you trying to say?"

"I'm saying," Eb replied, his voice calm now, steady, "that the flora and fauna in Africa don't fear man because they don't have to."

"And the snakes here?" Doc asked.

"Something must have changed," Eb said, whispering. "Something—the ecosystem, the forest—something changed so much that it altered the snakes' behaviors. I'm saying that here, just like in Africa, snakes now don't fear man."

Audio Transcript

Interview with Sheriff Jackson Fredrickson, concerning the Savage River Forest Tragedy aired on WMSC Maryland News

---

Interviewer: *You said in prior reports that you saw the security detail heading past you, correct?*

Sheriff Fredrickson: *That's right, sir.*

Interviewer: *But they were in civilian-style vehicles. How were you able to identify them?*

Sheriff Fredrickson: *Well, it wasn't hard. That up-armored six-wheeler they were driving? Stuck out like a dirt-covered glizzy. Looked like something out of one of those video games my nephew plays. Around here, we see security details pretty often. We're not clueless. They might as well have been driving a car shaped like a hot dog. That truck? It had "trouble" written all over it. You just knew someone with deep pockets had given them a job. Subtle wasn't their strong suit, that's for sure.*

Interviewer: *You also mentioned that you suspected they were heading toward Savage River State Forest?*

Sheriff Fredrickson: *It wasn't exactly a leap. We'd had protests, folks connected to the park losing their jobs. The whole economy around here's been knocked sideways. Then you've got Republican and Democrat leaders locking arms at protests—things were getting real strange. It wasn't just politics though. It felt like nature itself was shifting.*

Interviewer: *Nature shifting? What do you mean by that?*

Sheriff Fredrickson: *We had Sawyer Sallison—poor boy got bit by a copperhead, right in the middle of town. Now, copperheads don't usually slither into town like that. We've got snakes, sure, but not where folks live and breathe. It felt like something was off, like the world we knew was changing. And when a kid dies on your watch...* [pauses, voice tightens] *you start thinking a little deeper about what's going wrong.*

Interviewer: *Do you think this is tied to global warming or climate change?*

[Interview pauses, Sheriff Fredrickson crosses his arms.]

Sheriff Fredrickson: *Look, I'm not here to talk politics. My job's to protect people, keep 'em safe, keep 'em working. What I care about is life—human life. Whether it's the economy or nature itself going haywire, my responsibility is keeping folks alive. Sawyer's death was one too many, and the folks out in that truck? I wasn't about to let them add more to that number if I could help it.*

Interviewer: *But you've mentioned how this shift in the local ecology has affected everything, and you're suggesting there's more to it than just bad luck. Isn't this an issue tied to broader environmental changes?*

Sheriff Fredrickson: *I'm not blind to what's going on in the world, but when you've just buried a twelve-year-old boy, the last thing folks need is a debate on global warming. People's lives are sacred, and I'm not going to let politics muddy that truth. Right now, I don't need to be fanning the flames of that argument. I need to be focusing on the fact that something's changing around here, and people—real, living people—are getting caught in the middle.*

Interviewer: *But science could help us understand what's happening—*

Sheriff Fredrickson: *Science has its place, and it's supposed to help us, not distract us from the people we're supposed to protect. You want this interview or not? Like I said, yes, I saw that security detail rolling through our county. They weren't hard to spot. We're not too far from DC Metro, so seeing those up-armored trucks isn't unheard of. But putting the pieces together? That's where it took some thinking.*

Interviewer: *Thinking? What led you to connect the dots?*

Sheriff Fredrickson: *I knew those boys were heading west. Pipe-hitters looking for trouble. And based on everything that'd been happening, it didn't take a genius to figure out where they were going: Savage River State Forest. A lot of out-of-towners don't understand the land like we do. We live and breathe it, and if you've been around here long enough, you know when something's not right. I had a bad feeling about them, and I was right.*

Interviewer: *A bad feeling? You mean you thought they were in danger?*

Sheriff Fredrickson: *Absolutely. It wasn't about being tired of outsiders. I pity those boys—pity 'em because I knew they were walking straight into something bad. They didn't know the land, didn't know what was lurking in those woods. I should've stopped them, and maybe—just maybe—I could've saved them from the hell they found.*

Interviewer: *So, you believe their lives were at risk the moment they entered Savage River State Forest?*

Sheriff Fredrickson: *Look, around here, life's fragile. You can feel it when you lose someone young, like Sawyer. You understand real quick how sacred life is, how easily it slips away if you're not paying attention. It's a heavy thing, protecting folks. But the folks in that truck? They didn't know what they were walking into. And it wasn't just me knowing the land; it was me knowing that sometimes, people get in over their heads, and they pay for it with their lives. And that's why I'm sitting here, thinking about what I could've done differently.*

PART II

CHAPTER 1

"What are we doing?" Eb said, his voice gruff as Appalachia tugged at the steering wheel.

"We're eating on the local economy," Appalachia said, a hint of a smile tugging at his lips.

Eb scowled. "You serious? We're sittin' in this Avtoros, and you wanna roll up to some diner? Full of people?"

Before Appalachia could respond, Cora's voice cut through the air. "It's not your call, Eb," she said, arms crossed, her gaze steady.

Eb clenched his jaw. "A diner?" he said, letting the incredulity bleed into his tone. "In this beast of a machine? In an Avtoros Sham—"

"I'm the one paying the bills, remember?" Cora said.

Eb felt his frustration rising. The thought of being surrounded by people, their noise, their chatter, made his skin crawl. "I'll grab a protein bar from the gas station," he said.

"No, you won't," Cora said. "You're part of this team, and I want you contributing to the Maryland economy, not hiding away."

Eb scratched his chin, feeling the heat of frustration flare. "So, what? You wanna pretend like stuffing our faces at a diner makes a difference? You think that's helping anyone?"

"It helps the people who live here," Cora said. "The farmers, the families who run these places. It's the least we can do. Or do you just care about yourself?"

Eb gritted his teeth. "I care about not getting suffocated by strangers while I eat," he said. "What, you expect me to sit there and pretend to enjoy myself while you play Mother Teresa?"

"You have to see beyond your own needs, Eb," Cora said. "I know it's uncomfortable for you. But there's a world beyond this truck. These people... they matter."

Eb's eyes flickered toward the Taco Tico, its neon colors garish against his irritation. The fluorescent fuchsia and mint screamed '80s nostalgia, almost making him laugh. But the tension still pulsed in him.

"Fine," he said. "Do what you want."

"Alright," Jacques said from the front. "I'll be back in an hour."

Eb shoved his laptop into his bag and unbuckled his seatbelt. The others were discussing restaurant choices, but he paid no mind as he walked down the street.

A flash of neon pulled his attention. "Is that a Taco Tico?" he said. The fluorescent pinks and blues reminded him of simpler times, when things weren't so complicated. He pushed the door open, the hum of old machines filling the air.

Sliding into the quiet, he pulled out his earbuds and cued up a track from The Cello Doll, trying to lose himself in the music.

When the crew member brought out the tray, the bright fuchsia plastic looked absurd against the worn-down restaurant. He stepped forward, but the cashier waved him down.

"Sir? That's not yours," the cashier said.

"What?" Eb said, yanking out one of his earbuds.

"That's hers," the cashier said, nodding toward the counter.

Eb's heart skipped. Cora. She took the tray, moving with that same smooth grace. Eb watched her, his mind racing. What is she doing here?

The cashier handed him his tray, and he retreated to the corner, resuming his music. But his eyes kept drifting toward Cora.

As if reading his thoughts, Cora appeared at his table. "Everyone else goes to a mom-and-pop restaurant," she said, "and you come to a fast-food joint."

"I came here to eat," Eb said. "What, you following me now?"

Cora shook her head. "No. I came here because it looked like you could use some company."

Eb clenched his fists under the table. "Yeah, well, I'm fine," he said. "I didn't ask for this."

"I know," Cora said. "But you need it."

Eb tightened his jaw, fighting back the urge to tell her to leave. He couldn't bring himself to do it. Not today.

“Fine,” he said again, still not meeting her eyes. “Stay. But don’t expect me to talk.”

Cora sat down across from him. Her bun, which had been tightly wound earlier, was now starting to loosen. A few strands of hair had fallen out, decorating her face. Despite the chaos in his mind, Eb felt his whole body grow warm—pulled in by those unbound strands of hair.

“I wouldn’t dream of it,” Cora said.

CHAPTER 2

Eb grimaced as Cora sat across from him in the retro-designed Taco Tico lobby. The bright, fluorescent colors clashed with the heavy tension between them. He couldn't focus on anything but the urge to plug in his earbuds and shut out the world, but he couldn't afford to offend his boss either.

Cora watched him closely, hands folded on the table. "So," she said softly, "Eerie Ebenezer."

Eb stiffened at the sound of his podcast name on her lips. "What, did you get caught up in some gossip channel? What else do you know?"

Cora's eyes narrowed slightly, but her tone stayed neutral. "I've heard things."

Eb felt a flash of suspicion, but he kept his face neutral. He wasn't about to let her rattle him. "Yeah, well, I talk about a lot of things," he said. "Weird stuff. Things most people think are a joke."

"You don't?" Cora asked, leaning forward just a little, her voice even but with a hint of curiosity. "Think it's a joke, I mean."

Eb studied her, trying to figure her angle. "No. I don't." His voice came out harsher than he intended, but he didn't care. He was used to people laughing off his work, and something about her even bringing it up put him on edge.

Cora's gaze softened, just a touch. "I wasn't laughing."

Eb's brow furrowed. "Then why'd you bring it up?"

Cora paused, as if weighing her next words. "I brought you onto this job for a reason," she said, her voice calm but serious. "I don't just pick people at random."

Eb frowned. "Chose me? What are you talking about?"

Cora didn't look away. "You know your stuff. You're thorough. And I think you can see things other people can't."

Eb sat back, crossing his arms. The compliment felt strange, coming from her. He wasn't used to people valuing his skills, especially not people like her. "I didn't think this gig was about my... expertise," he said, letting the word hang in the air, heavy with sarcasm.

Cora didn't flinch. "It is. More than you realize."

There was something in her tone that made him pause, something almost... personal. But she didn't elaborate, and Eb wasn't about to ask. Instead, he tried to brush it off. "Well, whatever you think I know, I'm just here to do the job. Keep my head down. Get paid."

"Fair enough," Cora said, her expression unreadable. "But just so you know, I think you're more capable than you give yourself credit for."

Eb blinked. The words landed harder than he expected. He had been prepared for judgment, condescension, maybe even dismissal. But not that. He shifted uncomfortably, unsure how to respond. "Right," he muttered, not fully convinced. "Sure."

Cora offered him a small smile, though it didn't quite reach her eyes. "You don't have to believe me. But I believe in what you're doing."

Something about the way she said it caught him off guard. There was a weight to her words, a sense that maybe she knew more than she was letting on. For a split second, he wondered if she had listened to his podcast—if maybe she knew more about him than she wanted to admit. But he quickly pushed the thought aside. It wasn't possible. She was just trying to keep the peace, keep him on track.

Still, the tension lingered between them, unresolved but quieter now. Eb ran a hand through his hair, trying to process what had just happened. The bitterness inside him hadn't faded, but it was harder to hold onto it now. "Thanks," he muttered.

Cora nodded, but didn't press any further. "You're welcome, Eb."

He didn't correct her nickname this time. Instead, they both sat in silence. The buzzing lights of the Taco Tico hummed overhead. The unspoken weight between them not fully lifted but no longer suffocating.

CHAPTER 3

The silence between Eb and Cora was thick as they walked from the Taco Tico back to the Avtoros Shaman. The neon colors of the commercial restaurants clashed with the weight of Eb's thoughts. He shoved his earbuds in, hoping The Cello Doll could drown out the tension. But Cora's presence beside him remained impossible to ignore. Her calm, measured pace made him feel even more on edge.

He glanced at her. Of course, no sign of stress or fatigue. She was always composed, always in control. He pulled his jacket tighter and tried to focus on the music, but every step they took only heightened his discomfort.

They reached the Avtoros Shaman. Eb swiped the team key through the lock, opened the door, and let Cora inside first. He followed, sliding into his seat and leaning back, retreating into his usual isolation, his earbuds playing softly.

The rest of the crew returned about half an hour later. Eb felt his nerves rising as the vehicle filled with conversation. His music couldn't drown out the voices. Jacques was talking to Dirty Chap, who looked a little more jittery than usual.

"You ever notice how every situation has something off about it?" Jacques said. "You've got to stay sharp, anticipate. That's the only way you get through things."

Dirty Chap fidgeted with his gear. "Yeah, guess so."

Appalachia hummed to himself as he settled into the driver's seat, trying to keep the mood light.

Eb adjusted the settings on his laptop, ensuring the GPS signal remained strong. His fingers moved quickly, but the sense of unease stayed with him.

"That's strange," Eb said, staring at the screen.

"Appalachia," Eb called out, pulling out his earbuds. "You heard of any protests in the area recently?"

Appalachia glanced over his shoulder. "Protests? Not really. Why?"

Eb tapped the screen. “Connectivity’s weak. I’ve heard of environmentalists cutting down towers. Wonder if that’s what’s happening.”

Appalachia frowned. “Cutting towers? That’s no small feat. They’d need serious equipment, not just some clippers. And they’d have to mess with the wiring... seems unlikely.”

Jacques leaned in. “I don’t know. It could be anything. But we should check it out before we start guessing.”

Eb sighed. “Yeah, maybe it’s just the area. Could be nothing.”

Cora looked over at him. “Anything else on the map?”

“No,” Eb said, “but it feels off.”

Before anyone could respond, the Avtoros Shaman jerked violently to the side. A loud thud echoed through the cabin, followed by a sharp screech. Appalachia gripped the wheel, fighting to steady the vehicle. The SUV swerved, the weight shifting as the brakes engaged.

“What was that?” Cora asked, calm but alert.

The vehicle slowed to a stop, the systems adjusting to the sudden halt. Eb’s heart pounded, the sharp adrenaline rush still buzzing in his chest.

“We must have hit something,” Appalachia said, rubbing his chest.

Eb glanced at his screen, trying to focus. “The back right tire... it’s jammed up.”

“Deer tend to run into vehicles,” Appalachia said, catching his breath. “It might’ve gotten caught in the axle. We’ll need to check for damage. Could’ve bent something on the suspension or alignment.”

“Yeah,” Eb said, “but deer don’t scream.”

Appalachia’s face went pale. Jacques leaned forward.

“We better take a look,” Jacques said. “Let’s figure out what’s going on.”

Eb stepped into the cool night air, flashlight in hand. The metallic scent hit him right away—sharp and unsettling. He moved toward the back of the Shaman, shining the beam of light on the rear tire. Appalachia followed, his steps slower now.

“Was it a deer?” Appalachia asked.

Eb crouched down, his flashlight illuminating the twisted wreckage. He stood up, his expression neutral.

Dirty Chap shuffled closer. “What’d we hit?”

Eb turned toward the group. “It’s not a deer.”

Dirty Chap froze, his eyes wide. Jacques stepped up beside him.

“What is it?” Jacques asked.

Eb motioned toward the tire. The flashlight beam revealed the mangled body of a mountain lion, its limbs twisted around the axle. Blood had soaked the ground beneath it.

Appalachia frowned. “That... that’s not good. Something hit it hard enough to get tangled in the drive train. Could’ve messed up the steering link.”

“Not a deer, but this doesn’t make sense,” Eb said. “Why would a mountain lion run straight at us?”

Cora knelt beside the body, inspecting the fur and injuries closely. She stood and wiped her hands on her pants.

“It wasn’t running in a straight line,” Cora said. “Look at the way its paws are scraped. It was trying to change direction, but... something forced it off course.”

Dirty Chap glanced around nervously. “What would make a lion run like that?”

Jacques looked at the scene with quiet focus. “Sometimes there are things we can’t explain right away. But we keep going. We stay alert.”

Eb glanced back at the mangled body, unease gnawing at him. Whatever had made the lion run into them wasn’t something they could dismiss.

Eerie Ebenezer Podcast Episode – "Florida's Chaotic Ecosystem with Dr. Franklin Mazzagalli"

Eerie Eb: *Alright, welcome back to Eerie Ebenezer's Paranormal Podcast, folks. Today's episode isn't about ghosts or aliens, but something just as wild happening in the real world. We're talking about Florida's ecosystem being turned upside down, and who better to discuss it with than Dr. Franklin Mazzagalli. He's written Florida—The Chaotic Ecosystem, and man, does he have some insights into what's going on with the Burmese python invasion. Dr. Mazzagalli, thanks for joining us.*

Dr. Mazzagalli: *Glad to be here, Eb. Florida's got more than its fair share of challenges when it comes to invasive species, and the pythons are right at the top of that list.*

Eerie Eb: *Let's get into it. One thing that's been blowing my mind is the impact this invasion is having on, like, everything. We've got stories of alligators getting more aggressive, even attacking people more. What's going on there?*

Dr. Mazzagalli: *It's definitely concerning, Eb. While it's difficult to draw a direct line between the python population and a rise in alligator attacks on humans, there are some notable patterns we can't ignore. What we're seeing is an increased level of competition between alligators and pythons, especially for food. This competition can push alligators out of their normal territories or put them under more stress, leading to more unpredictable behavior.*

Eerie Eb: *So, you're saying the pythons are messing with the gators' hunting grounds?*

Dr. Mazzagalli: *Precisely. In areas where pythons have become established, they're preying on many of the same species that alligators rely on—raccoons, birds, small mammals. With their food sources depleted, alligators may become more territorial or aggressive, especially when they have to compete with another apex predator like the python. This can lead to alligators venturing closer to human habitats in search of food or, in some cases, becoming more defensive and hostile when they encounter people.*

Eerie Eb: *And when you say 'more defensive,' are we talking about increased attacks?*

Dr. Mazzagalli: *That's right. We've seen some evidence suggesting a rise in alligator attacks in areas heavily affected by pythons, though it's important to be cautious with those claims. The correlation is still being studied, but it's clear that competition between these predators is disrupting the natural order, making alligator behavior more erratic. Encounters between humans and gators are increasing as a result.*

Eerie Eb: *Man, that's crazy. So, it's not just that pythons are eating everything, they're pushing gators into areas they don't usually go, which means more attacks on people.*

Dr. Mazzagalli: *Exactly. Alligators are opportunistic predators. If their usual prey is scarce, they're more likely to take risks, and that sometimes means coming into closer contact with humans. And, unfortunately, that can lead to more attacks, especially in urban or suburban areas where gators are already present but now feel more pressured.*

Eerie Eb: *Okay, so it's not just gators. You've mentioned before that there's also been a spike in road fatalities—more deer getting hit. How's that connected to the pythons?*

Dr. Mazzagalli: *That's another ripple effect we're seeing, and it's just as troubling. Deer, like other prey species, have been reacting to the presence of pythons in ways we haven't seen before. Pythons are ambush predators, and while they aren't chasing deer down in the traditional sense, the sheer threat of them has caused deer to act more erratically. In python-heavy areas, deer are fleeing more frequently and in unpredictable directions. This is leading to an increase in deer running onto roads and highways, which has, unfortunately, caused more vehicle collisions and fatalities.*

Eerie Eb: *So, the deer are basically panicking?*

Dr. Mazzagalli: *Yes, that's a good way to put it. They're in a heightened state of vigilance, constantly on alert for threats. This leads them to flee at the slightest disturbance, and in some cases, that means darting onto roads they wouldn't typically approach. The result has been a significant rise in road collisions in certain areas, with more fatalities reported each year.*

Eerie Eb: *Man, that's intense. We're talking about real human lives lost here, just because these animals are trying to get away from pythons.*

Dr. Mazzagalli: *That's right. The road fatalities aren't just numbers—they're lives lost due to an ecosystem that's been thrown into chaos. And it's not only deer; other species, like raccoons and even birds, are showing unusual behaviors as they try to adapt to the new predator in town.*

Eerie Eb: *So you've got alligators attacking more, deer running into traffic, birds changing where they nest—this whole thing is a mess. I mean, what do you think's gonna happen next?*

Dr. Mazzagalli: *It's hard to say exactly where things will go from here, but what's clear is that the longer we let the python population grow unchecked, the worse the fallout will be. We're already seeing significant damage to the ecosystem, and it's affecting everything from animal behavior to human safety.*

Eerie Eb: *This whole situation sounds like it's spiraling, man. You've said it in your book—Florida—The Chaotic Ecosystem—this isn't just an animal problem anymore. It's way bigger than that.*

Dr. Mazzagalli: *The truth is this, that place has become an ecological battlefield...and lives have been lost in the process.*

CHAPTER 4

Eb stood frozen. He stared at the lifeless mountain lion entangled in the wheel of the Avtoros Shaman. Its bloodied fur and twisted limbs spoke of an indescribable violence. The wilderness had its own rules—unforgiving and harsh—but this felt wrong, out of place. He couldn't shake the uneasy feeling creeping up his spine.

Why would a mountain lion run into the road? Eb thought.

"Yo, dawg, I don't think this image is ever leavin' my mind," Dirty Chap said, forcing a nervous chuckle in a weak attempt to break the tension.

Jacques stepped closer, inspecting the scene. "Looks like this is more than just a hit-and-run." He nudged the lion with his boot, his expression thoughtful but calm.

"No," another voice said. Marcus Mattucks stepped forward, his arms crossed. "But you were right to bring me along."

Eb turned toward Marcus, who studied the mountain lion with a frown.

Jacques sighed. "You're telling me this thing was endangered?"

Marcus hesitated, crouching down to examine the body. "It depends."

There was a collective groan from the group. Eb couldn't help but let out a dry laugh, already sensing where an impending dialogue from Marcus chalked full of legalese.

Trigger-pullers, a team made up of strong personalities, hated the ambiguity of legal talk.

"What does that even mean?" Jacques asked.

"We don't know exactly what species this is," Marcus said. "Mountain lions aren't endangered, but if this is a Florida panther—"

"Then we've got a problem," Eb finished, trying to stay focused despite the mess of thoughts swirling in his head.

Marcus nodded. "We'll need to report this if it is."

Jacques shook his head, his frustration evident. “So, you’re saying we need to contact the game warden, park police—someone.”

“We might have to,” Marcus said, “depending on what the wildlife authorities say.”

“We’re here for my sister,” a firm, determined voice interrupted.

Everyone turned as Cora stepped forward, arms crossed, her gaze fixed on the group. “I don’t care how many cougars we hit. I’m here to find my sister.”

Jacques raised a hand, trying to calm her. “Cora, this isn’t about the mountain lion. We just need to make sure we’re not getting into trouble. No one’s saying we aren’t focusing on your sister.”

“If you don’t deal with this the right way,” Cora shot back, her voice cold, “you’ll get sued.”

“Boss,” Marcus said, glancing at Jacques.

Jacques turned to him, clearly weighing his options, but before the conversation could continue, Eb’s senses kicked into gear. The smell of the dead animal hung in the air, but something else caught his attention—something subtle, a distraction that pulled him away from the gore.

Eb’s eyes drifted back to Cora. Her rigid posture remained, but something about her expression didn’t match the steel she was showing. Despite her strength and sharp tone, there was something in her eyes—something vulnerable, almost fragile.

For a second, Eb thought he saw her eyes welling up, a glassy sheen forming as tears threatened to fall. He hesitated.

“You alright?” Eb asked, his voice softer than he intended.

Cora turned to him, her hardened expression breaking slightly before her features tightened again. She seemed to collect herself before answering. “I’m fine.”

Eb felt a wave of self-consciousness wash over him. “You sure?”

Cora gave a soft chuckle, shaking her head. “Thanks for asking. I didn’t expect that from you.”

Eb scratched his head, unsure how to respond. “Well... you seem upset.”

"Of course I'm upset," Cora sighed, the firmness in her face softening for a brief moment. "We're wasting time, and my sister's out there."

Eb glanced at the mountain lion, then back at her. "Your perfume smells a lot better than that thing."

Cora rolled her eyes but didn't seem offended. "That's flattering, Eb."

"That's not what I meant," Eb said, chuckling awkwardly. "It's just... that scent, it's been chasing me since you got here. What is it?"

"It's called Loveville," Cora said, a faint smile touching her lips.

"Loveville," Eb muttered, feeling the heat rise to his face. "Like the town?"

Cora nodded. "Probably the rhubarb you're smelling."

Before Eb could respond, Jacques called out, "Eb, over here."

Eb looked back to see Jacques standing near the front of the vehicle, motioning for him to come over. Reluctantly, he left Cora and walked toward his boss.

"We're leaving part of the team here," Jacques said, crossing his arms.

Eb's eyes lit up, the thought of a break from this chaotic job lifting his spirits. "What do you mean?"

"We'll leave some of the team to handle this," Jacques explained. "We don't want the legal issue to hold us up. If it turns out that thing is endangered, we'll pay the fine, but the rest of us are moving on."

"So, you want me to stay back here?" Eb asked, trying to keep the excitement out of his voice.

Jacques shook his head. "No, Eb. I need you with Cora."

Eb's face fell. "Wait, what? You're telling me I'm babysitting the heiress?"

Eb stopped as he heard Cora's voice behind him. She cursed under her breath, her footsteps heavy as she walked toward the truck. Eb turned and saw her moving past him, her shoulders tense, her face set in anger.

"Cora, wait," Eb called out.

She stopped but didn't turn around, her voice cutting through the night air. "I was wrong about you, Eb. There's no humanity in you."

Eb felt a knot form in his stomach. "I didn't mean—"

"There was no 'save the cat' moment," Cora continued, her tone colder than before. "Just indifference. You care about this job and your podcast, but when it comes to actual people, you're just cold."

Without another word, she walked away with a finality that echoed in Eb's chest.

Jacques stood beside him, his arms crossed. "That didn't go very well."

"She's wrong," Eb muttered. "I do care. But what she doesn't realize is that being human just makes me another kind of animal."

CHAPTER 5

Eb shuddered as Jacques' gaze lingered on him. With slow, deliberate movement, he turned his head toward his boss.

"Walk with me," Jacques said.

They walked a few paces, the sounds of the team fading behind them, the cold air pressing down on Eb's chest. His stomach twisted, anxiety creeping in.

"Why don't you like Cora?" Jacques asked suddenly. "Or, as you put it, 'the heiress.'"

"I—"

"You think she's just a nepo-baby, right?" Jacques' voice was sharp. His eyes narrowed into slits.

"I wouldn't call her that—"

"Well, let me tell you something. She's not." Jacques crossed his arms, his expression hard. "She earned her spot on this team. I get where you're coming from, though. I don't like nepotism either. But Cora? She's here because she's good at what she does."

Eb nodded, slowly at first, then more rapidly, unsure of where the conversation was heading.

"And that's why we don't like you."

Eb blinked, caught off guard. "What do you mean?"

Jacques stepped closer, his voice lowering. "You think you're here because you earned it? You're here because of your uncle. Gray Beard. He vouched for you."

Eb's body tensed as the truth slammed into him. His uncle, Alan "Gray Beard" Myrddin—a man with a legendary career in the military—had secured his spot. Not his skills. Not his talent.

"My uncle...?" Eb muttered, his mind racing.

Jacques nodded, his expression both angry and resigned. "You've been coasting on his name. And while I respect Gray Beard, I've been questioning you since day one."

Eb tried to speak, but Jacques cut him off.

"And Cora?" Jacques continued, his tone hardening. "She respects you. She wanted to meet 'Eerie Ebenezer,' the guy from the podcast. But you've treated everyone here like they're beneath you. You've acted like we're the supporting cast in your little drama."

"That's not—"

"It is," Jacques snapped, his eyes blazing. "You've been walking around like you're above this, like this is some favor you're doing us. Newsflash: you're not. You're here because your uncle believes in you. And right now? You're letting him down."

The words hung heavy in the cold air. Eb felt the weight of them settle in his chest, leaving him off balance.

Jacques stepped back, shaking his head. "You think this is just about your podcast or some paycheck? It's not. You either step up, or you step out. Right now, you're on thin ice."

Eb looked downward, with the palpable feel of Jacques' disappointment.

CHAPTER 6

Eb sighed, his breath visible in the cold air. He stood in front of Jacques, feeling small under his boss' gaze. Jacques said nothing, his eyes still burning into Eb, waiting.

"What do I need to do?" Eb asked, his voice barely above a whisper.

"Get out of your Peter Pan syndrome," Jacques said. "You need to grow up. Fast."

Eb's stomach tightened. He knew what was coming next.

"You're not getting out of this trek," Jacques said. "You'll hike with the team, and when this is done, we'll reassess."

Eb nodded, his mind racing. He wasn't afraid of the hike, but this wasn't just about the physical journey. It was about stepping up, proving himself. But right now, he wasn't sure he could.

"And one more thing," Jacques said, his voice soft but firm. "You need to fix things with Cora. Now."

Eb swallowed, knowing Jacques was right. He'd crossed a line with Cora, and if he didn't fix it, things would only get worse.

Eb approached the Avtoros Shaman, his nerves on edge. To his relief, Cora hadn't entered the vehicle yet. She stood outside, arms crossed, her face set in stone.

"Cora," Eb started, his voice low and unsure. "Can we talk?"

She didn't move, her eyes cold as she turned to face him. "What's this about, Ebbie?"

Eb hesitated. He hadn't expected her to be this angry. He thought he could just apologize and move on, but the words stuck in his throat.

"I... messed up," he finally said. "I shouldn't have said what I did. I was wrong."

Cora stared at him, her silence heavier than anything she could've said.

"Why now?" she asked, her voice calm but filled with skepticism.

Eb struggled to find the right words. "Because... I didn't realize how much I screwed up until Jacques talked to me. I didn't mean to disrespect you. I was... I was out of line."

Cora crossed her arms, her posture stiff. "And you think that fixes everything?"

Eb shook his head. "No. But it's a start."

She didn't respond immediately, just watching him, assessing. Eb's heart pounded as the tension grew.

"It's not too late for you to make things right," she said finally. "But this? It's not enough. Not yet."

And with that, she turned and climbed into the Shaman, leaving Eb standing alone in the cold.

CHAPTER 7

The Avtoros Shaman rumbled to a halt on the forest's edge, its massive tires crunching over the gravel as the engine idled. The forest's edge, cloaked in creeping darkness, loomed large—its tall, twisted trees standing as ancient sentinels standing against the starless sky. The shadows slithered and swayed in sinister shapes that shifted silently as the night swallowed the last remnants of daylight.

"Well," Appalachia said, twisting behind the steering wheel, "it's been real and fun, but not real fun."

Eb barely registered the humor, his thoughts tangled in the dense undergrowth of anxiety and unease. As he stood, the heavy blanket of self-consciousness pressed down on him. The Shaman had been more than just a vehicle—it had been their fortress, their last barrier against the unfathomable unknown that lay within the forest's depths. Now, with its engine silenced, they were exposed, vulnerable to the inscrutable gaze of the wilderness.

Eb and the others crawled out, leaving Appalachia in the driver's seat. Eb glanced over at Cora, who was already peering out the window, her fierce eyes narrowing as she scanned the thickening woods ahead.

Eb and the others then gathered their weapons from the gun rack. They adjusted their equipment, donning gloves, tightening ammunition belts and necessary equipment, and donning eye protection.

"This is as far as we go on wheels," Eb said, his voice calm but carrying the weight of the decision they were about to make. "From here, we're on foot."

Cora's gaze flicked to him, a trace of surprise breaking through her usual composure. "On foot?" she echoed as if the idea was foreign.

"You didn't want us to stop, remember?" Eb asked.

"Of course," Cora said, "I just thought—"

"Wait..." Eb said. "You have a weapon, right?"

Cora's eyes widened in surprise.

"No," Eb said. "You brought one or were issued one, correct?"

"I—I have my Glock," she said, "but I don't have the license for concealed carry."

"Well, ma'am," Eb said, "our attorney is back there, so we have plausible deniability. Plus, I'd feel a little better if you were better secured."

"I have a holster," she started.

"Dirty Chap," Eb called out, turning behind him, "Cora needs your assistance."

"I got you," Dirty Chap said and jogged up to her position.

Cora crouched, her fingers fumbling as she retrieved the uncharged Glock and the holster from her pack. Dirty Chap knelt beside her, helping her secure the holster to her hip with a swift, practiced efficiency. He then charged the weapon with a cold click of the slide locking into place.

Muleskinner nodded as he adjusted the sling of his rifle. "Alright," he interjected. "The sign's out there, but it won't wait for us."

The others continued to manipulate their gear, the sounds of zippers and buckles filling the air. From his peripheral vision, Eb saw Cora's hesitation—brief but unmistakable. He looked up at the forest ahead, its shadowy depths seeming to pulse with an ancient, unknowable rhythm.

"You sure about this?" Eb asked, trying to keep his tone steady, though a slight tremor betrayed his unease.

Cora slung her pack over one shoulder, glancing back at him. "Sure as I've ever been."

Eb smiled in acknowledgment and offered his balled hand for a fist pound.

"Respect," he said as she knocked her knuckles against his.

She gave a slight nod.

"And what about dinner?" Cora asked.

Eb turned to face her. The question came out half-heartedly, an apparent attempt to lighten the mood, but Eb sensed an edge of uncertainty.

Eb cracked a faint smile, one that barely touched his eyes. "Dinner will come and go, Cora. What matters is that we see tomorrow."

There was a pause as Cora let his words sink in. Then, with evident determination, she adjusted her grip on her assault pack strap and squared her shoulders. “Alright then. Lead the way.”

Then, together, they stepped into the sinister shadows of Savage River State Forest.

The group ventured deeper into the forest. Above them, the thick canopy grew thicker into an almost solid ceiling of green. Despite its thick canopy, light did break through the cover, casting long, creeping shadows. Eb suddenly halted, holding up his hand. The others stopped, their breaths shallow in the quiet of the woods. There, pressed into the soft earth, was a footprint—deep, and unmistakably human.

Muleskinner knelt beside it, his keen eyes studying the impression. “Looks like we’ve got some company,” he said, running a gloved finger around the edge of the print. “That looks fresh to me.”

Standing slightly behind, Cora glanced at the print and then back at the group, smirking. “Yeah, but I know shoes.”

Muleskinner looked up, raising an eyebrow. “A shoe aficionado; you’re a ‘sneaker head?’”

Cora knelt beside the print, took out her phone, and snapped a picture. “No... I’m a woman. I’m telling you that hussy borrowed my shoes without asking.”

“Wait,” Muleskinner said, “your sister might be hurt, how can you talk about her like that?”

“All things considered,” Cora stood up, “she’d be more offended if I didn’t call her that.”

Muleskinner blinked, then let out a low chuckle. “Good to know.”

Muleskinner stood up, signaling for the group to resume their hike. Muleskinner stayed next to the sign. With the brief exchange breaking the tension, the hike continued.

Their sign-cutting led them further into the thickening trees until the air around them grew heavier, the scent of charred wood wafting toward them. They stopped abruptly as they reached a clearing—a once vibrant part of the forest now reduced to a blackened despair. The jet-colored stains of ash. The sand-like remains of mighty trees that now smoldered in smoke.

"That's strange," Eb said and pointed into the melee. There—scattered among the debris—were ball-shaped stones. Eb came forward, kneeling beside them.

"What is that?" Cora asked.

Eb said nothing, focusing his vision on the rock. He picked it up. He dropped it as his fingers touched cold, wet material.

"Ugh," he said and stared down at his hands.

Bits of scarlet stained his flesh. He raised his hands to his nose, smelling the substance.

"I knew it," he said, recognizing the blood's peculiar, sweet, iron-like smell.

"What does that mean?" Cora asked. "Why are those rocks lying *on top* of the ashes?"

Eb remained silent, no longer blurting out answers but instead thinking of the best way to communicate with his employer.

"Everything else is all dusty," Cora pointed at the rocks. "Those look clean."

Eb wanted to tell her good job and compliment her on her powers of observation. But while that would be accurate, it wouldn't be appropriate.

"What...what does that mean?" Cora asked, a slight quiver in her voice.

"It means," Eb said, staring down at the blood-covered rock, "somebody was out here throwing rocks."

CHAPTER 8

Eb wiped his hand on his pant leg, the crimson stain smearing across the fabric.

"Rock throwing?" Cora asked.

Eb looked up from his squatted position, studying Cora. "Yes...rock throwing."

"This is weird," Muleskinner said.

"Yeah," Cora muttered, "weird."

"But the trail ain't dead," Eb said, pointing at the soil. "Still sign."

"What's the plan?" Dirty Chap asked, his voice barely above a whisper, as if speaking too loudly might summon whatever lurked in the darkness.

"I think," Muleskinner said, "we follow Eerie Eb."

Eb looked up. He could feel his own disbelief.

"What?" Eb asked.

"Cora, ol' Gray Beard," Muleskinner said, "they must have seen something that none of us else saw. You picked up that sign, and you look like you know what you're talking about. I can manage, you keep us on point."

Eb's mouth gaped open, and he looked from Muleskinner to Cora. Despite the evident peril, Cora allowed a smile to creep across her face.

"I-" Eb started.

"Come on, man," Muleskinner said, "I just complimented you... don't drag this out...get us on point."

Eb took a deep breath; a smile crept across his face despite his frustration. His mirth faded in an instant as he felt the blood on his fingers.

Those aren't pebbles, Eb thought to himself.

"Wait," Eb said, sliding his assault pack from his back. He unzipped it and dug his hands inside.

"What's up, Eerie?" Muleskinner asked.

"That's for her," Eb said, handing Muleskinner a sleek, forest-colored Pro-Tec helmet.

"Understood," Muleskinner said and handed it back to Cora.

"It looks like a helmet for a skateboarder," she started.

"Just take it," Muleskinner said.

"But what about him?" Cora asked.

"Eh," Muleskinner shrugged and tapped his first finger on Eb's head, "I say that head of his is harder than Kevlar."

"Thanks," Eb said, laughing as he zipped his assault pack.

"Lead us out, Eerie," Muleskinner said.

Muleskinner signaled with his hands, and the others followed course, standing up and assuming an excellent tactical stance.

"I was wrong about you," Cora said, closing next to Eb.

"Oh yeah?" He didn't look up at her but continued to study the ground. "How so?"

"*This*," she said, as she adjusted the buckle on her helmet, "is your save the cat moment."

Eb looked up to reply, but she had already left.

Then, further into the darkness, the company continued.

CHAPTER 9

"Deeper into the darkness," Eb said, following the foot traffic into the Savage River State Forest. The towering trees stood as ancient sentinels; their gnarled branches intertwined to form a nearly impenetrable canopy. Only slivers of sunlight managed to pierce the thick foliage, casting fleeting, freckled patterns on the forest floor. "It's horrible that something so beautiful has been tainted by such tragedy," Eb mused, his gaze sweeping the forest's shadowy expanse. The ground beneath their feet was a spongy mat of pine needles and decaying leaves, exhaling the rich, earthy aroma of the wild. Shadows danced with each step. The team moved with tactical precision; their senses stretched taut.

"*Che cazzo?*" a voice suddenly cut the air. Eb's head snapped around, heart jumping into his throat. Doc stood frozen, arm outstretched, pointing into the trees.

"What is that?" Eb narrowed his eyes, straining to see.

A dark shape materialized from the shadows—an eerie, abandoned structure half-hidden by the forest.

"That's a house?" Eb asked, voice low.

"Might be one of Aristov's hideouts," Doc muttered, his tone laced with unease.

The house seemed to rise out of the ground, its dark stone walls covered in symbols that made Eb's skin crawl. Shattered windows gaped open, their jagged edges reflecting faint rays of light, giving the place an abandoned, dangerous feel. The roof shimmered black, and even the weak sunlight struggled to penetrate its surface.

Eb crouched, scanning the area. "Something's wrong here. Too quiet."

Ahead, Cora stopped abruptly. Her voice wavered as she stared ahead. "Dahlia... the tracks..." Her words barely reached him.

Eb's pulse quickened as he saw her body tense. She took a step toward the house, panic radiating from her.

"Whoa," Eb said, stepping forward and grabbing her arm. "Wait."

"My sister's in there," she snapped, trying to pull away from him.

"We haven't cleared it," Eb said, his grip firm. "You rush in, and something happens, that's on me. I'm not carrying that."

Cora glared at him, her eyes wild, but she didn't pull away again. She clenched her jaw, her fingers twitching against the side of her helmet. For a second, Eb thought she'd argue, but then her gaze fell to the ground.

"Trust me," Eb said quietly. "We'll go in, but together."

Before she could respond, Dirty Chap's heavy hand clapped down on Eb's shoulder.

"Yo, dawg," Dirty Chap said, his voice solid. "Muleskinner gave the green light. Let's roll."

Eb exhaled, feeling the knot in his chest loosen slightly. Dirty Chap's calmness had a way of grounding him.

"Alright," Eb said, and together the team approached the house.

CHAPTER 10

Eb's stomach churned as they reached the house. The air thickened, the foul stench of decay and sulfur crawling into his lungs. His skin prickled with unease.

Accidental gave a quick nod toward the door, which hung slightly ajar. "No need for a breach," he whispered.

Eb signaled the team to stack up, moving in with their weapons raised, careful and precise.

The moment Eb crossed the threshold, the stench slammed into him like a wall. Sulfur mixed with the metallic tang of blood. His nostrils flared, and he clenched his jaw to keep from gagging. Glass and debris littered the floor, crunching underfoot as they moved further in. Dark stains smeared the walls—old blood, grime, and something else he didn't want to think about.

"This place reeks," Eb muttered, keeping his rifle up.

Dirty Chap grunted. "Whatever happened here, it wasn't pretty."

The room opened into a large space, its stone walls rough and cold. Torches mounted on the walls flickered, casting shadows that danced with every move they made. In the center, a massive table lay overturned, its wood splintered and worn.

Doc's voice came from the far end of the room. "Got one."

Eb moved quickly, his heart thudding in his chest. Doc knelt beside a figure slumped against the wall. As Eb neared, his breath caught in his throat. The man's face was a nightmare—eyes gouged out, blood leaking from the empty sockets. His hand dangled at his side, missing most of its fingers.

"Heee!" the man wailed, his voice barely human.

The sound chilled Eb, freezing him in place. The man rocked back and forth, his breath shallow, his head jerking violently.

"Here!" the man screamed, his voice cracking. *"It's still here!"*

Eb's stomach twisted, the pitiful sight gnawing at his insides. A sharp, acrid smell hit him next—like rotten eggs, burning his nose. Something wet and thick splattered on his arm. He glanced down, confused, before his gaze shot upward.

Then Eb saw it.

Clinging to the beams above, a massive figure watched them. Its red eyes glowed with a primal rage.

"A-a-ape," the maimed man managed.

Yes, Eb thought, *it is.*

The creature had the thick, muscular body of a chimpanzee, its limbs gripping the beams with ease. Auburn fur clung to its torso, but its face—bare and twisted—resembled a terrifying fusion of a chimp and an orangutan. It bared its fangs, long and sharp, yellowed with age and blood. The sulfurous stench rolled off it in waves, making Eb's stomach churn. Something about it felt ancient, like an ancient relic suddenly thrust into the present.

Eb's hand trembled as he raised his weapon, finger tightening on the trigger.

"He's saying it's still here!" Doc yelled.

BANG! BANG!

Eb fired, but the creature moved in a blur, leaping across the room.

CRASH!

It collided with Muleskinner, the impact sending a sickening sound through the room. Muleskinner hit the ground hard, pinned beneath the creature's weight.

"There!" Eb shouted, adjusting his aim.

The creature's red eyes gleamed as it snarled, its fangs dripping blood. It kicked off Muleskinner's body and launched itself toward the wall. Its powerful limbs scaled the stone as gunfire rang out, but it moved too fast. In one final bound, it crashed through the shattered window and disappeared into the forest.

Eb dropped beside Muleskinner, his heart pounding. Blood pooled around his throat. His body lay still, lifeless.

"He's dead," Eb whispered, the weight of the words crushing him.

CHAPTER 11

"Che cazzo!" Doc's voice shook. "What was that thing?"

Eb didn't respond, his mind racing. "Where's Cora?"

He sprinted outside, eyes scanning the dim clearing. Under the darkening sky, Cora stood frozen, pale as a ghost. She stared into the distance, unmoving.

"Cora!" Eb called, his voice cracking.

She didn't respond, her body stiff, her eyes wide. Eb rushed to her, grabbing her hand. Her skin felt cold.

"Cora, what happened?" he asked, his voice low, almost pleading.

She didn't look at him. Her gaze remained distant, lost in whatever she had just seen. Eb's chest tightened, the sight of her like this unnerving him in a way the creature hadn't.

"Yeah," he said quietly. "I saw it too."

CRACK!

A rock smashed against the wall behind them. Instinct kicked in, and Eb pulled Cora with him toward the door.

"Get inside!" he shouted, dragging her with him.

They barely made it through the door before Eb slammed it shut. His heart raced, his grip still tight on his rifle.

"Friendly! Friendly!" Eb called out, scanning the room.

Doc's face was pale, his eyes wide with fear. "What the hell was that thing?"

"I think we all know," Accidental said, stepping forward, calm but serious.

"We need a plan," Eb said, catching his breath. "Doc, where do we start?"

"We still have to clear this house," Accidental replied.

Doc's voice rose, frantic. "Cora, you brought us here. What was that?"

Cora stood by the door, her eyes downcast, avoiding their gaze. Eb stepped closer, his pulse still racing.

"You know something," Eb said, his voice rough. "Talk."

Cora's eyes flicked up, locking onto his. "You, of all people, know what we're up against."

Eb's brow furrowed. "What are you talking about?"

Accidental stepped in. "She's saying you saw it. You know what that thing is."

Doc took a shaky step toward her. "Did you know? Did you know what we were walking into?"

Eb's mind raced, the weight of the situation sinking in. He glanced at Muleskinner's mutilated remains, then back at Cora, the realization hitting him hard.

"You picked us because of me? Is he dead because of me?" he asked, his voice breaking.

Cora didn't meet his eyes. "My sister... I thought you could help me find her."

Eb sank to one knee, his breath ragged. *This is on me.*

Accidental reloaded his weapon, his face grim. "We know what we saw. Now let's finish this."

Eb slowly rose to his feet, hands trembling as he reloaded his rifle. "Yeah. We saw it. We saw Sasquatch."

CHAPTER 12

Eb stood in the oppressive air of the great dining hall. The overwhelming scent stung his nostrils. His eyes swelled with his tears, as he realized that stench—that particular scent as the sharp, metallic scent of Muleskinner's blood. The tension gnawed at him. Each of his teammates wore their emotions openly—anger, fear, and anxiety painted on their faces.

Doc, Dirty Chap, and Accidental stood clustered together, while Cora sat hunched near the back, pale and visibly shaken. Her fingers twisted with evident nervous energy, her gaze darting from her teammates to the floor.

Eb broke the silence, his voice low but steady. "We've got two options. We either cut our losses or go after Dahlia."

Dirty Chap leaned forward, arms crossed. "Is that even an option?" His voice was rough, filled with skepticism. "What makes you think Dahlia's even alive after what just happened?"

Eb glanced at Cora, whose hands tightened into fists. He could see the guilt eating at her, but her desperation outweighed it.

"Have you heard of the Cincinnati Zoo?" Eb asked, his voice measured. "And Harambe?"

"Yeah, dawg," Dirty Chap grunted. "The internet blew up with that meme storm."

"That's not the point," Doc interjected, crossing his arms, eyes serious. "Eb's making a reference. Harambe didn't kill that child. He grabbed him—abducted him."

Eb nodded, catching Cora's gaze. "Exactly. There's history of Sasquatch abductions dating back over a hundred years. They take people—sometimes alive. Dahlia could still be out there."

Dirty Chap shook his head. "Yo, is yous really suggestin' we waltz into the same nightmare that took Muleskinner? That's how people get killed, Eb."

Accidental leaned against the doorframe, his arms crossed as he watched the conversation unfold. "Statistically speaking, the longer we stay, the worse the odds get. We don't have the resources to handle a search and rescue mission, especially not one against... whatever that thing is out there. The rational move is our departure."

Cora flinched, her eyes darting toward Muleskinner's body, which lay motionless on the ground. The sight of it seemed to twist something inside her. Eb noticed her hands trembling slightly, but her jaw tightened. She wouldn't break, not yet.

"She's not dead," Cora said, her voice cracking. She stood up slowly, her legs shaky but her determination apparent. "We have to try. My sister... I know she's still alive. She's out there somewhere. That thing—like Harambe—it's taken her, but she's alive." Her eyes pleaded with the group, but when she looked at Eb, her voice softened. "Please, Eb, you've seen things like this in your research."

Eb felt her hand brush against his arm. It was a small touch, but it sent a wave of uncertainty through him. He caught the desperation in her eyes, but also something else—an unspoken belief that he was the one who could save Dahlia. The guilt she carried was etched into every word she said, but her determination was fierce, almost tangible.

Accidental shook his head. "Cora, I get it. I really do. But the math here doesn't add up. We've lost a man. We've got limited supplies, and we don't have a way to communicate with anyone. That thing—whatever it is—already took down one of us. We need to focus on surviving, not on chasing ghosts."

Doc sighed heavily, his gaze landing on Muleskinner's body. "I hate to say it, but Accidental's right. My job's to preserve life, not throw it away. We're on our own out here. No backup. No medevac if things go south again. If we go after Dahlia and get pinned down, I don't have enough supplies to patch us all up."

Eb watched as Cora's face twisted with pain at their words. She opened her mouth to speak, but Doc continued.

"This isn't a rescue op, Cora. This is survival. We're already one man down, and I don't know how many more we can afford to lose."

Dirty Chap leaned forward, rubbing his temples. "We're here because of you, Cora. You dragged us into this, and you didn't tell us the full story. If we'd known about all the disappearances, about whatever monster's out there... things might've gone differently."

Cora looked down, her shoulders slumping under the weight of her guilt. "I didn't know it would be like this. I didn't... I didn't think it would get this bad," she said, her voice wavering. "I'm sorry. I should have told you. But I need you to help me find my sister."

Eb's chest tightened. He understood the fear in his teammates, and he knew the logical course was to leave. But there was something about Cora—something in her relentless determination and the way she looked at him—that pulled at him. She believed in him.

"We have a choice," Eb said, pacing as he tried to gather his thoughts. "I get it—we're low on ammo, down a man, and we have no idea what's really out there. But if there's even a chance that Dahlia's alive, I can't just leave her."

"Then you're insane," Dirty Chap muttered. "We're not prepped for this. Muleskinner got ripped apart like he was paper."

Cora reached out again, her fingers brushing Eb's arm. "I believe we can do this. I believe you can do this."

Eb stopped pacing, her words settling into him. He could feel her trust in him—her belief that he was the right man for this—that her sister's earthly salvation depended on him.

"Doc, Accidental, Dirty Chap," Eb said quietly, "I'm not asking anyone to follow me. If you want out, I get it. But I'm going after Dahlia. I'm not leaving her behind."

Accidental sighed, rubbing his forehead. "You're making an emotional decision, Eb. But you're also a grown man, and I can't make this choice for you."

Doc crossed his arms. "I'm a doctor. I save lives, and I know when not to waste them. But if you're going... I'm in. Someone's gotta keep you alive."

Dirty Chap stood, slinging his rifle over his shoulder. "This is suicide, Eerie Eb. But if you're staying, I'm not leavin' you to fight that thing alone."

Eb looked at each of them, his heart heavy but resolute. He turned to Cora, who gave him a small nod of gratitude, though the guilt still lingered in her eyes.

"Anyone who stays," Eb said, "better be ready for a fight. Because whatever's out there... it's not gonna let us leave easy."

CHAPTER 13

Eb stood at the front of the room, his mind racing as the silence stretched. The mission was no longer in question—they were going after Cora's sister, Dahlia. But now, he could feel the weight of their collective gaze on him. The real question was hanging in the air: *Was he the right man to lead them?*

Dirty Chap leaned back against the wall, arms crossed, watching Eb carefully. "So, dawg," he said, his voice measured, "you got the knowledge on this thing, sure. But are you ready to take point?"

Doc glanced at Dirty Chap before looking back at Eb, a frown pulling at his lips. "Look, man, I know you've got the expertise, but this isn't some research expedition. People are gonna die if you mess this up. You ready for that weight on your shoulders?"

Eb shifted on his feet, feeling the tension in the room growing. He had the knowledge, sure—he'd spent years studying Sasquatch reports, piecing together stories and theories. But leading a team through Savage River State Forest, hunting a creature that had just torn apart one of their own? That was something else entirely.

Cora sat on the edge of a chair, her face pale and her eyes downcast. Guilt radiated off her in waves, but there was a quiet desperation in her, too. Her hand touched Eb's arm again, this time more deliberate. "I believe in you, Eb. I don't have a choice but to. My sister... you're the only one who understands what we're dealing with."

Eb felt her words hit him, but they didn't give him comfort. They only added to the weight pressing down on his shoulders. He wasn't ready for this. He hadn't signed up to lead. But the reality was, they had no one else. *No one else knew what they were facing.*

Accidental cleared his throat, arms crossed, eyes locked on Eb. "Statistically, it makes sense for you to lead," he said, his tone cool and analytical. "You're the only one with direct knowledge of this... creature. But that doesn't account for the fact that you've never led a mission like this. We're already down a man. I'm not interested in us becoming another statistic."

Eb met Accidental's gaze, his stomach tightening. "I know the risks," he said, his voice quieter than he intended. "I didn't ask for this, but I'm here. And if I'm the only one who knows how to deal with what's out there, then I'll lead. But I'm not pretending to be something I'm not."

Doc let out a heavy sigh, shaking his head. "Che cazzo... we're really doing this." He walked over to Muleskinner's body, glancing down for a moment. His voice softened as he spoke, though the edge of uncertainty lingered. "If you lead, you better make sure you can make the hard calls, Eb. We can't lose anyone else."

Eb swallowed hard, the reality of Doc's words sinking in. "I'll do what I can," he said, his voice a bit stronger now. "I know I'm not the guy who's supposed to be in charge, but right now, I'm the best shot we've got."

Dirty Chap nodded slowly, his expression unreadable. "You're not wrong, dawg. You know the thing we're hunting better than any of us. But we're not following you just because you're the 'expert.' You gotta earn that."

Cora stood, stepping toward Eb, her hand brushing his arm again. This time, she looked him directly in the eyes, her voice soft but firm. "You're the right one for this, Eb. You know you are. You don't have to pretend to be some big-time leader. Just... be the person who can save my sister."

Her words hit something deeper in him. Eb felt a shift. He didn't have to be the fearless leader they were looking for. He just had to be the one who knew what they were up against.

"I can do that," Eb said quietly, more to himself than to anyone else. He looked around the room at his team—at Doc's cautious eyes, Dirty Chap's guarded posture, Accidental's calculated expression. "We move smart. We don't take unnecessary risks. And we stick together."

Accidental nodded, his arms still crossed. "Sounds like a reasonable plan, but the margin for error is still small."

Dirty Chap stood straighter, adjusting his gear. “Alright, dawg. You take point, I’ll back you up. But you screw this up, and I’m out.”

Doc moved closer, his gaze hard but with a glint of reluctant respect. “You better believe if something goes sideways, I’m pulling everyone out.”

Eb met their eyes, feeling the gravity of their words. He wasn’t the fearless leader they expected, but he was the one they needed right now. “We’ll get through this,” he said, feeling the confidence build, though it still felt fragile.

“We head into Savage River in ten,” Eb added, taking one last look at Muleskinner’s body before stepping out of the room.

As he walked, he felt Cora’s eyes on him, her hand brushing his arm once more. She didn’t say anything, but the look in her eyes told him what he needed to hear: She trusted him, and that was enough.

The Unseen Foragers of the Forest - Witness Report

Interviewer: *Thank you for joining us today, Mr. Dickinson. Could you tell us a bit about your recent findings near Savage River Forest State Park?*

Dax Dickinson: *Absolutely. It’s been a strange few weeks. Everyone around here knows I’ve been tracking wildlife in Savage River for years. Still, recently, I stumbled upon a creature I’d never seen before—it turned out to be a Pika. Never seen those around here before.*

Interviewer: *A Pika, that’s quite unusual for this region, isn’t it?*

Dax Dickinson: *Oh, it’s more than unusual; it’s unheard of. Pikas are mountain creatures, you see, and this area is far from their natural habitat. I took the little guy to the local wildlife clinic to make sure I wasn’t seeing things.*

Interviewer: *And what did they say?*

Dax Dickinson: *They confirmed it, all right. It was a Pika. No doubt about it. The vet was as baffled as I was. They’re not native here, which makes you wonder how it ended up in Savage River.*

Interviewer: *There's been some talk about Heinrich Aristov's recent activities in the park. Has there been any connection?*

Dax Dickinson: *Heinrich? Yeah, he's been up to all sorts. Ever since he took over managing the park, there's been a lot of changes, not all of them good, mind you. Word is, he's been importing various species to boost the park's natural appeal, which sounds as crazy as it is illegal.*

Interviewer: *Do you think the Pika could be one of these imported species?*

Dax Dickinson: *Wouldn't put it past him. There's been a lot of hushed talks about shipments and unusual animals. If you ask me, Aristov's trying to turn the park into some sort of personal zoo.*

Interviewer: *And how do you feel about that?*

Dax Dickinson: *It's reckless. Introducing non-native species can wreak havoc on the local ecosystem. Who knows what kind of balance he's tipping with these actions?*

Interviewer: *There are also rumors that Pikas could be linked to larger predators. Any thoughts on that?*

Dax Dickinson: *You mean the Sasquatch stories? I've heard folks say that Pikas could be a food source for bigger things. If Sasquatches are real, and you're bringing in their food, who's to say you aren't inviting them closer to us?*

Interviewer: *That's a concerning thought.*

Dax Dickinson: *It is. Suppose Aristov is pulling strings behind these introductions. In that case, he might be setting us up for something we're not prepared to handle. All for what? A little more foot traffic in the park?*

Interviewer: *Thank you, Mr. Dickinson, for sharing your insights.*

Dax Dickinson: *I'm afraid it will draw in predators that are not normally found in this area. Just hope someone starts taking this seriously before it's too late.*

CHAPTER 14

The wind howled through the Savage River State Forest. Branches whipped to and fro, mercilessly beaten by the wind. Through this gust-torn environment, Eb led his team forward. His hands gripped the rifle tightly, the weight of Muleskinner's helmet heavy on his head. Eb had scrubbed the inside clean but hadn't had time to fully wash the outside, where four bloody fingerprints remained.

You're keeping me safe, Muleskinner, Eb thought, adjusting the chin strap, trying to block out the image of his friend's final moments.

He turned to check on Cora, who trudged beside him. Cora's vitiligo-patterned face was pale and Eb observed her breaths were shallow. Eb reached out, his gloved hand closing around hers for a brief moment.

"You alright?" he asked.

She nodded, her lips pressed into a tight line. Her eyes told a different story—fear and guilt painted in the lines of her face. Eb felt a knot tighten in his chest. Cora's pain was evident and she blamed herself for dragging them into it.

Before she could say anything, a sudden stillness fell over the forest. The air, which had been alive with the rustling of leaves and distant calls of birds, now felt thick and oppressive. Eb's stomach twisted.

Something's coming, he thought.

Suddenly, a rock flew through the air with brutal speed—*WHAM!*—slamming into Cora's chest, sending her sprawling backward into the dirt. She hit the ground hard, somersaulting before coming to a stop, her body still.

Eb's first instinct was to run to her, but he forced himself to stay focused, raising his rifle and scanning the treeline. "Ten o'clock, fifty meters!" he shouted, already taking aim.

The rest of the team reacted instantly, weapons raised as they opened fire—*BANG BANG BANG!*

A chilling scream echoed through the forest. Eb's heart pounded in his ears as the barrage of gunfire filled the air. The creature was close, but still hidden in the thick brush.

We got it, Eb thought, but there was no relief.

"Cease fire!" Eb called out, waving his hand in front of him. The gunfire stopped as quickly as it had started, leaving an eerie silence in its wake.

Eb's eyes darted back to Cora. She groaned, slowly pushing herself up, her hands trembling as she clutched her chest. "You okay?" he asked, moving toward her.

Cora nodded weakly, her breath ragged. "Thanks... for the vest," she whispered, her voice hoarse.

"Good thing you had it on," Eb said, feeling a strange warmth rise in his chest.

Dirty Chap stepped forward, rifle still in hand, his face a mixture of shock and adrenaline. "Yo, dawg, over there," he said, pointing.

Eb followed his gaze. His stomach clenched. A figure lay in the underbrush, half-covered by leaves and dirt. Smoke rose from its body.

It's dead.

They moved closer, weapons still at the ready, but Eb held up his hand, signaling them to stop. He stared down at the creature, trying to keep his composure. The Sasquatch lay motionless, blood pooling around its fur-covered body, its nostrils wide and exposed.

"It's a juvenile," Eb muttered.

Doc knelt beside the body, his face pale. "This... this isn't right," he said quietly. His hands hovered over the creature as if he couldn't bring himself to touch it. "*Che cazzo*... I thought we'd be fighting some wild animal, but this..."

"Man, it stinks," Cora said, stepping closer, her nose wrinkling in disgust. She reached out with a stick, gingerly poking the Sasquatch's exposed nostrils. "It's like a mix of sulfur and rotting flesh."

"Probably carnivorous," Eb said, trying to push past the unease. "Look at its body—wiry, built for hunting. Gorillas get bulky from eating plants, but chimps—"

"That thing—it's a monster," Dirty Chap interrupted. "That thing could've ripped us apart if it wanted."

Cora nodded, her face tight with fear. "It looks like a…a…misplaced memory."

"It's called 'pseudo-memory,'" Eb said. "You're scared of that thing, even though you've never seen one. The Inuit tells stories about the Tizheruk or Tshikha—monstrous snakes that hunt in the Arctic waters…their ancestors told those stories for survival. Flora, fauna—all of nature is dangerous. They knew their ancestors needed to fear it."

Doc stood, wiping his hands on his pants as though trying to rid himself of the filth of the moment. "This isn't just some cryptid. This thing was hunting us." His voice cracked, and he took a step back. "And we killed it."

"As you stated," Accidental said, "this was only a juvenile. If it was hunting, then there's a likelihood we'll encounter a fully matured one soon. The chances of surviving another encounter decrease significantly if we're not prepared."

Eb glanced at him, his stomach sinking further. *Accidental's right,* he thought, but the weight of the situation wasn't fully registering. He felt like he was moving on autopilot, reacting rather than leading.

Cora took a shaky breath, her eyes fixed on the dead Sasquatch. "How many more are there?" she whispered. "Could they be…hunting us?"

Eb hesitated for a moment, his finger brushing against the trigger of his rifle. Then he raised the barrel to the creature's head, aiming carefully.

BANG!

The sound echoed through the forest, and the group flinched. The Sasquatch's head jerked back, revealing its sharp, tusk-like teeth. Smoke drifted from its open mouth.

"Just making sure," Eb said, trying to ignore the tightness in his chest.

For a moment, the group stood in silence, each of them processing the reality of what had just happened. The juvenile Sasquatch lay dead at their feet, but the forest around them felt more dangerous than ever.

Eb looked at Cora, who stood close to him, her face pale but determined. He saw the guilt in her eyes, the fear for her sister, but also the hope that she was still out there.

"I'll get her back," Eb said quietly, meeting her gaze. "We'll find Dahlia. I promise."

Cora nodded, her hand brushing against his arm again, lingering for just a moment longer than necessary. "I believe you," she whispered, her voice thick with emotion.

But as Eb turned away, leading the team deeper into the forest, he couldn't shake the feeling that he wasn't the right man for this job. Not yet.

Eerie Ebenezer Paranormal Podcast

Special Guest Danny Vendramdt, Author of *Them Against Us: How We Defeated The Neanderthals*

(Interview taken prior to the events in Savage River Forest State Park)

Eerie: *Danny, thanks for making the trip from Australia to the United States! I'm so glad I was able to catch you at the con, and I'm grateful you were willing to speak with us.*

Danny: *Cheers, mate! Stoked to be here. Bloody oath, what a long haul it was, but ya gotta do what ya gotta do, eh? Ain't every day you get a crack at yappin' on about Neanderthals and all that good stuff on a Yank podcast, mate!*

Eerie: *Alright, Danny, I know you've done a lot of research on Neanderthals. You published the book, Them Against Us: How We Defeated The Neanderthals and if you know me, I talk a lot about cryptozoology and generally 'weird topics.' So, right off the bat, what do you think about Sasquatch?*

Danny: *Fair dinkum, mate, you're straight into it, ain't ya? Classic Yank, no muckin' around, eh?*

Eerie: *Hey, us Americans don't have a 38-hour work week, we gotta get down to business.*

Danny: *Yeah, fair go, I can't bite the hand that feeds me, eh? You Yanks saved our arses in WWII, against the Japs. If it weren't for you lot, we'd be chattin' in Japanese right now!*

Eerie: *Well, you gave us Natalie Imbruglia, so I'd say we're even.*

Danny: *Ah, crikey! Love that Sheila too, but c'mon, mate, that's like comparing a stubby of VB to the bloody Sydney Opera House. We're talkin' national bloody sovereignty here!*

[Both laugh]

Eerie: *Alright, let's get back on track. You've looked over some of the Sasquatch evidence. What's your take?*

Danny: *Righto, well, the evidence isn't off the charts, but it's not nothin', ya know? When it comes to Sasquatch... well, Yeti is a whole different kettle of fish, mate.*

Eerie: *Different how?*

Danny: *It's gut instinct, mate. Science says there's no such thing as these creatures, but even science talks about things like the Bongo mystery apes in Africa, right? Like their version of Sasquatch. And I reckon... well, I reckon our gut's got a bit more say than we give it credit for.*

Eerie: *Wait a sec, Danny, are you sayin' our gut instincts are enough to prove Bigfoot exists?*

Danny: *Nah, mate, not sayin' that at all. What I'm on about is this: Neanderthals, right? They've been turned into cuddly, misunderstood fellas. Like, we paint 'em up like your local postie or something. But they weren't like us, mate. They were carnivores, hunters... predators. Same reason tourists here get gored by bison—'cause they think those big buggers are just like oversized cows.*

Eerie: *Still not followin', mate. Where's Sasquatch in all this?*

Danny: *What I'm gettin' at is this, right? Us modern humans—especially in the comfy Western world—we've gone soft. We think nothin' means us harm. We make excuses for violent blokes and shame anyone who defends 'emselves. But Neanderthals, mate... they weren't humans like you and me. They were bloody apex predators. The same way we ignore danger now, folks back then probably did too. Till they ended up in some Neanderthal's belly!*

Eerie: *So what, you're sayin' Sasquatch is a throwback to Neanderthals?*

Danny: *Not exactly. I'm sayin' there's this deep, old knowledge in our guts, mate. Take your Inuit folks up in Alaska. They've got stories 'bout bloody snakes! Now how do folks in the frozen north get snake legends?*

Eerie: *Right, I think I'm followin' you now.*

Danny: *Too right, mate! I'm sayin' our ancestors—our bloody survival instincts—kept this knowledge, right? Like the Inuit with the snakes. We might not see it, but we bloody well feel it. Sasquatch? Maybe. Something like it? Definitely. Mate, it's not just science... it's what's baked into our bones. We see a vast forest, or some deep wilderness, and our gut's screamin', "Something's out there!"*

CHAPTER 15

"Here you go," Eb said, handing Doc his knife.

Doc shook his head and drew a longer, black tactical Kukri blade. The weight of it in his hand seemed to momentarily still the tremor in his fingers. He knelt by the juvenile ape, staring at it with wide eyes.

"*Che gazzo!* This is the craziest thing I've ever done," Doc muttered, his breath uneven.

Eb smirked, trying to lighten the mood. "Oh, c'mon, Doc, you've dealt with worse. What about all those gnarly STDs you've had to handle?"

"Yeah," Doc said, "and you know where the king of STDs came from?"

"AIDs?" Eb asked.

"Human immunodeficiency viruses," Doc said. "And you know where that terrible disease came from?"

Eb sighed. He knew the answer—Pan troglodytes—Congolese Chimpanzees between the Sanaga and Congo Rivers. Eb knew there was more to it than that, but he understood what Doc was saying. Blood diseases. 2020 had taught the world just how dangerous a folded prion could be.

Eb shifted uncomfortably, his gaze flicking to the dead juvenile. "Yeah, well, we're all vaccinated for the usual crap. What's one more pathogen?"

Doc's sharp gaze shot up. "This isn't a joke, Eb. Diseases like this... they're time bombs. And we're walking straight into the blast radius."

There was a brief silence as the weight of Doc's words hung in the air. The team wasn't just fighting monsters—they were fighting nature itself, and nature didn't play fair.

"You ever see someone die from something they never saw coming?" Doc asked suddenly, his voice softer, more distant.

Eb frowned, caught off guard by the shift in tone. "What do you mean?"

Doc took a deep breath, his hand pausing on the Kukri. "I grew up in a rough neighborhood. Baltimore. One of those places where bad things happen, and you just learn to live with it." He swallowed hard, eyes distant. "One of my closest friends, Luis... we were kids, messing around on the street like we always did. One night, a drunk driver came barreling down the block. Luis never saw it coming. Hit him so hard..." Doc trailed off, his voice thick with emotion. "He was gone before I could even try to help."

Eb remained silent, unsure how to respond. He wasn't great with this kind of thing emotions, tragedy. But he could tell this weighed heavy on Doc, even after all these years.

"After that, I swore to myself I'd save people," Doc continued, his voice gaining strength again. "But you know what really inspired me?"

Eb shook his head no.

"The medic," Doc said, "the one that came to Luis. Luis was pretty much dead—died on impact—even back then, as a dumb kid I could see it. But the medic, he kept doing CPR on Luis. Right there in front of me, he stayed on the stretcher as they put him in the ambulance. And despite the death that shook my world—in that moment—I found hope."

"Hope?" Eb asked. "Your friend just died."

"But that medic," Doc said, "he knew the truth. He knew what I needed to see. I needed to see the ray of hope despite the adversity. Death had consumed my friend, but still the paramedic pushed. He knew the truth—the truth about lost causes."

"What do you mean?"

"The thing about lost causes," Doc said, "is that they're the only ones truly worth the struggle."

"But you fought against this mission," Eb said. "Said it wasn't worth the risk."

"Yes," Doc said. "Because my job was to take care of you. You're my leader—but your job was to look after her—look after Dahlia—and even if the mission is lost, the world will know that we cared for her."

Eb nodded slowly, unsure of what to say. "I never knew you thought like that."

Doc managed a small, sad smile. "Not the kind of thing you talk about over beers and there hasn't been a chance for that since we've been on this trail."

Eb didn't know what to say. He could feel the knot in his throat tightening as he watched Doc carefully slide the Kukri into the Sasquatch's flesh, making the first incision.

Suddenly Doc stopped.

"Here," Doc said and his hand—still free of blood—went to his neck. He tugged at a chain, pulling it from beneath his tactical vest. A small pendant gleamed in the low light—a worn image of Saint Jude Thaddeus. Doc held it up, staring at the pendant for a long moment before turning to Eb.

"Saint Jude," Doc said quietly, his fingers brushing the necklace. "I've carried this since Luis died—after I saw that paramedic working. He's the patron saint of lost causes. And right now... well, this feels pretty hopeless."

Eb felt a pang of awkwardness as Doc extended the necklace toward him. He wasn't Catholic. His Church of Christ upbringing didn't exactly endorse the whole saint thing, and the idea of taking it felt wrong, but the look in Doc's eyes stopped him.

"Take it, man," Doc said softly, his voice almost pleading. "I've carried it long enough. It's gotten me through some dark places Maybe it'll help you now."

Eb hesitated, the weight of the pendant feeling heavier than it should. Slowly, Eb reached out, his hand trembling slightly as he accepted the necklace.

The metal felt cold in his hand—it carried a weight of hope, faith, and desperation. Eb could see the same struggle in Doc's face, the way he fought to keep everyone alive.

"Doc, I don't—" Eb began, his voice thick with uncertainty.

"I know," Doc cut him off gently. "I get it. But just keep it with you. You don't have to believe in it, just... hold onto it. For me."

Eb nodded slowly, feeling a strange sense of comfort despite the unease bubbling in his chest. He slipped the necklace into his pocket, his fingers brushing against the cool metal.

Doc exhaled, returning his focus to the creature before him. "Well," he said, his tone lighter now, though still laced with tension. "Whatever lessons we're learning here, we're not forgetting them."

Eb forced a chuckle. "I tell people that on my podcast all the time—you might regret listening, but you won't forget it."

Doc smirked but didn't say anything, the weight of the moment still lingering between them. He took a deep breath and made the first cut into the Sasquatch's body, his hands moving with surgical precision.

As the blade slid through the fur and flesh, Eb looked away, his mind racing. He couldn't shake the image of the pendant, the weight of it in his pocket, and the story behind it. This mission was different now. It wasn't just about survival—it was about something deeper, something that tied them all together in ways they hadn't anticipated.

We're not just fighting monsters anymore, Eb thought.

Eerie Ebenezer Podcast, Special Guest Dr. Bryan Harrison

Eerie Ebenezer: *Thank you so much for coming on the show, Dr. Harrison.*

Bryan Harrison: *Please, just call me Bryan.*

Eerie Ebenezer: *Alright, Bryan, I'm pumped to have a tenured professor here—so proud you're reppin' Goucher University.*

Bryan Harrison: *Actually, I'm not here representing Goucher University. I'm trying to present myself as an individual from the academic world... and I just happen to be a big fan of your show.*

Eerie Ebenezer: *That's a weird distinction, man.*

Bryan Harrison: *Well, I don't want the world thinking Goucher is out there declaring the existence of Sasquatch, ghosts, or any of the other things you talk about.*

Eerie Ebenezer: *Ah, a disclaimer, I get it. [Pauses, speaking in a dramatic voice] Let it be known that Goucher University does NOT encourage belief in Sasquatch.*

Bryan Harrison: [Laughing] *We encourage cynicism—not skepticism, but research. And you know, I've been told that 'Squatching' is a gateway drug to academic research.*

Eerie Ebenezer: *Really?*

Bryan Harrison: *Yeah... that's what the university public affairs team worked to convince us of before I came on the show.*

Eerie Ebenezer: [Laughs] *So, your university wants you engaging with the public, but your academic heads want you to avoid Sasquatch?*

Bryan Harrison: [Laughing] *That's exactly how it went.*

Eerie Ebenezer: *Well, the good news is, I didn't bring you on to ask about Sasquatch... at least, not today. I've read you and your wife's book on dogs, but I'm also interested in your research on chimpanzees.*

Bryan Harrison: [Chuckling] *Yes, and Sasquatch is also a gateway drug for interest in chimpanzees as well.*

Eerie Ebenezer: [Laughing] *Your marketing guys told you that too?*

Bryan Harrison: [Shaking his head] *No, I've seen it firsthand. Duke University's primatology program is full of students who were first drawn to the field because of Sasquatch legends.*

Eerie Ebenezer: *That's wild. You're a regular listener, huh? We mostly hit paranormal stuff, but sometimes we get into other cool things—like language, Muay Thai, guerrilla warfare... you know, stuff to keep people on their toes.*

Bryan Harrison: *Oh, I know your show, Eerie. You've got a great mix of topics.*

Eerie Ebenezer: *Sweet, sweet. So, I read in one of your papers that you've seen some crazy stuff with chimps—like they actually seek revenge?*

Bryan Harrison: [Leaning forward] *Well, 'revenge' is a human term. As an academic, I have to be careful how I phrase things. Chimpanzees, like all animals, have instincts, reactions—*

Eerie Ebenezer: [Cuts in] *But you look like you've got more to say...*

Bryan Harrison: [Takes a deep breath] *But... what I've seen, the horrors I've watched these creatures inflict... If you ask me, I'd say...* [Voice dropping to a serious tone] *yes... they seek revenge.*

CHAPTER 16

Simultaneously, while Doc skinned the Sasquatch, Eb wandered over to where Accidental was surveying the forest floor. Eb looked skyward as a few shafts of light broke through the swaying canopy above, freckling the ground around them.

"You ready to make the Seabees proud?" Eb asked, trying to break the tension.

Accidental shook his head, a half-smile creeping across his face. "A few days ago, I figured you were just some Nepo baby with a Bigfoot obsession."

"Obsession?" Eb clutched his chest dramatically, feigning a wounded heart. "You cut me deep, man."

Accidental chuckled. "You know what I mean, Grunt. Your uncle's lucky to have stuck you on the team. Now here I am, asking for your help—crazy how things change." He paused, giving Eb a glance. "So, what's the plan?"

"Trip fall," Eb replied.

Accidental rubbed his finger across his upper lip, his brow furrowed in thought. "Trip fall? You're taking me back to my Boy Scout days, Grunt. Aye, aye, I got you," he said. "But you know, statistically speaking, traps like this work about fifty percent of the time. Guess we're flipping a coin."

Eb raised an eyebrow. "That's better odds than I expected."

"Well," Accidental said, leaning in closer as he worked, "we're like the canary in the coal mine, except this time the equation's got too many unknowns. It's just a matter of which of us hits zero first."

With the e-tools they brought in their rucksacks, both men began to dig. They worked in silence, the scrape of shovels mingling with the sounds of the forest. A few shafts of sunlight broke through the swaying canopy above, freckling the ground around them. As they dug deeper, Cora watched from a short distance away, her eyes lingering on Eb.

"I can help," she said, stepping forward, her voice edged with determination.

Eb handed her a long, gnarled tree limb, motioning toward a nearby rock. "Sharpen this. We're gonna need punji sticks."

"Punji?" Cora arched a brow and crossed her arms.

"Haven't you seen that John Wayne movie? The one about Special Forces?" Eb asked, continuing his work.

Cora let out a dry laugh, setting to work on the branch. "Do I look like a John Wayne fan to you?"

Eb glanced up briefly, a grin pulling at the corners of his mouth. "Hey, even Stalin was a John Wayne fan."

"Well, I'm neither Stalin nor a Wayne fan," she said, holding the stick.

"What?" Eb asked, his voice full of mirth. "Every rich kid I know claims to be a socialist."

"Ah, yes," Cora said, her voice maintaining his mocking humor. "We just don't want you middle-class kids climbing up the ladder of the social hierarchy our parents handed down to us."

"That why you hate the oil business too, right?" Eb asked. "Because it made too many poor people rich?"

"Well, Eerie," Cora said, "the way your team talks, you're more of a Nepo baby than I am. And yes... I might have used my blessings to understand social causes, but some may say that's better than studying whatever you studied."

"Ouch," Eb said, smiling.

"Hey," Cora said, "I said 'some' people. I'm not talking about me. In all honesty... I'm a big fan of Eerie Ebenezer."

The compliment caught him off guard. Instead of confidence, an overwhelming feeling of imposter syndrome struck him. His heart thudded against his chest with a hummingbird-like rhythm. Blood hammered against his veins.

Was he really cut out for this? The weight of Muleskinner's helmet on his head weighed heavy against him. He closed his eyes, trying to calm himself. And then when he opened them—he saw her.

Cora.

Listen to her, Eb thought.

Her compliment had caught him off-guard, but her smile…her smile strengthened him.

Maybe he was starting to earn his place here. Maybe.

"So," Eb said, shifting awkwardly, "about those John Wayne movies."

"What about them?" Cora asked, still focused on sharpening the stick.

"If we get out of here," Eb said, glancing at her again, his tone lighter than the tension that hung over them, "I'll introduce you to the Duke myself. Might even make a fan out of you."

Cora's lips twitched, her eyes narrowing, as if in mock suspicion. "Is that your idea of a date, Ebenezer, or am I supposed to file harassment paperwork after this?"

Eb froze, the humor draining from his face as he fumbled for a response. "Uh... a date?"

For a heartbeat, Cora's expression remained unreadable. Then, the corners of her mouth softened, breaking into a warm smile. The contrast between her vitiligo-inked skin and the white of her teeth gleamed in the fading light.

"If we survive this," she said, her voice gentler now, "I'd love to."

Accidental's voice broke through the moment, his tone more serious. "Alright, Grunt, punji sticks are in place. But you know, this is like building a house out of matchsticks and hoping the wind doesn't blow."

Eb chuckled, shaking off the awkwardness. "Yeah, but if it works, we'll have something to show for it."

Accidental stood, wiping his hands on his pants. "That's what I like about you, Grunt. You're willing to play the odds, even when they're stacked like a deck of cards in a West Virginia poker game." He paused, glancing at the trap they'd set. "Let's hope Lady Luck's feeling generous today."

Eb glanced over at Accidental, appreciating the man's mix of practicality and grit. He wasn't just a math-and-data guy; there was something deeply rooted in him—Appalachian through and through. Even when the odds weren't in his favor, he'd dig in and make it work.

"Thanks," Eb said, his tone quieter now. "For trusting me."

Accidental shrugged, giving him a sideways glance. "We'll see if that trust is well-placed. But... I think you're the right man for this job, even if it's the craziest one I've ever seen."

"This is definitely unprecedented," Eb said.

Accidental paused. “And hey, fifty-fifty odds aren’t too bad. Better than trying to solve a quadratic equation with only half the variables.”

“I’m not exactly sure what that means,” Eb said, shaking his head, “but I’ll take it.”

CHAPTER 17

The skinned Sasquatch lay exposed in the clearing, its lifeless body twisted unnaturally. The stench of blood hung heavy in the air as Eb and his team hunkered down, their weapons trained on the surrounding forest. The tension in the Savage River State Forest was palpable, every rustling leaf making their fingers twitch, but they couldn't afford to waste bullets—not yet.

"It's coming," Eb said.

The forest echoed with the sounds of something large crashing through the underbrush. Shadows flitted between the trees, moving with terrifying speed.

"It's closer," Eb said, his voice tightening.

The Sasquatch leapt from branch to branch, its massive body bending the trees under its weight before launching off again. It moved with a disturbing agility, its power evident in every leap. The ground shook with each impact.

"Dio mio, it's fast!" Doc said, his breath coming in short bursts.

The beast hit the ground, its bipedal motion shifting to a bear-like gallop as it barreled forward, closing the distance in seconds. The team braced for impact, their hearts hammering in their chests.

Eb's eyes widened as he aimed his carbine, beads of sweat trickling down his neck. The Sasquatch slowed, sniffing the air, then crouched over the juvenile's corpse. Its fingers dug into the flesh, ripping at the remains.

"Now," Eb whispered.

The team held their breath as the Sasquatch brayed—*hoot-hoot-hoot!*—its terrible cries reverberating through the forest. The sound sent shivers down Eb's spine. The monster lifted the juvenile's body above its head. The blood dripped down its face as it smiled—a grotesque, fanged grin.

"What's it doing?" Cora whispered, her voice trembling. "Doesn't it realize it's one of its own?"

The Sasquatch hooted again, louder this time, shaking the body like a grotesque trophy.

"I can't watch this!" Doc said, standing up and leveling his weapon at the beast. He fired a warning shot, but it was too late.

The Sasquatch snapped its head toward Doc, its scarlet eyes gleaming. Before anyone could react, it lunged.

"Doc, no!" Eb screamed as the creature grabbed Doc in one massive hand and yanked him forward. The others fired, but the shots missed as the Sasquatch, still clutching the juvenile's body, tumbled into the pit.

CRACK!

The ground gave way, the trap finally springing, and both the Sasquatch and Doc disappeared into the abyss. Eb's heart pounded in his ears as he sprinted to the edge, peering into the pit below.

"Doc!" he shouted, panic rising in his chest.

Down below, the Sasquatch writhed, impaled by the sharpened punji sticks. Blood oozed from the wounds, but it still fought, its massive hands clutching Doc's leg as he struggled to break free.

"Doc!" Eb yelled again.

With a sickening crunch, the Sasquatch finally sagged, its strength giving out as the life drained from its body. Doc, gasping for breath, kicked the monster's hand off and scrambled back, leaning against the side of the pit, panting.

"Get him out!" Cora said, her voice cracking with relief.

Dirty Chap and Accidental rushed forward, their faces pale as they lowered a rope down to Doc.

"Doc, you good?" Dirty Chap called, his usual bravado replaced with genuine concern.

Doc grabbed the rope with shaking hands, wincing as he pulled himself up. "Good?" he said, his voice full of stress but laced with humor. "That thing nearly made *spaghetti* outta me."

Accidental grinned despite the tension. "We'll get you out of the pit first, Doc. Then we'll talk numbers."

As Doc climbed out, Dirty Chap clapped him on the back, laughing in relief. "Man, I thought we lost you! You're tougher than you look."

"Yeah, well," Doc said, still catching his breath. "I've been in worse scrapes, but this? This takes the *cannoli.*" He glanced back at the pit. "I think I'll be seein' that thing in my nightmares for a while."

"Get your bearings, Doc," Eb said. "We'll check on you in a second."

As the others crowded around Doc, Eb knelt at the edge of the pit, staring down at the Sasquatch. The creature's blood pooled beneath it, its massive body impaled on the sharpened sticks. But even in death, it looked monstrous—its fanged grin frozen in place, eyes still wide open in rage.

Eb felt a shiver run down his spine as he stood up. "That thing didn't come back to save its young," he muttered to himself, "it came back to feed."

Cora stepped beside him, her hand resting on his arm. "What do you mean?"

Eb pointed to the juvenile's mangled body in the dead Sasquatch's grip. "It wasn't here to protect it. It was here to eat it."

Eerie Ebenezer Podcast, Special Guest Dr. Bryan Harrison [Continued]

Bryan Harrison: *If I may, I'd like to take a moment to step back and reconsider the broader context.*

Eerie Ebenezer: *About what exactly?*

Bryan Harrison: *Ecology and the role of animal sciences in shaping our understanding of ourselves and the natural world.*

Eerie Ebenezer: *Go on.*

Bryan Harrison: *What I'm specifically referring to is a broader cultural tendency. As Americans, we have a peculiar habit of self-criticism. We declare ourselves to be the greatest nation, but that proclamation often serves less as a statement of pride and more as a provocation.* We're the greatest country, and yet this is how we address homelessness? We're the greatest country, and these are the individuals we elevate in our presidential elections? *This reflexive critique permeates many aspects of our societal consciousness, including our engagement with science.*

Eerie Ebenezer: *So, we turn ourselves into the bad guys?*

Bryan Harrison: *Precisely. And not just our national allegiances but even our own species. We do not celebrate humanity's lunar exploration. No. Anthropocentrism in scientific discourse often casts humanity as the perennial antagonist—whether we are disrupting ecosystems, overfishing oceans, or contributing to climate change. Take Peter Benchley, for instance.*

Eerie Ebenezer: *The novelist?*

Bryan Harrison: *Correct. Benchley, the author, spent the latter part of his life in deep regret, believing that his work had contributed to an irrational fear of sharks, which in turn allowed predatory fishing practices, particularly in the Pacific, to go unchecked. From a conservationist perspective, this regret is not unfounded. However, speaking as both a member of the scientific community and a human being, I would argue that our moral obligations ought to prioritize the well-being of our own species.*

Eerie Ebenezer: *This is a shift in the episode, Bryan. You got my attention.*

Bryan Harrison: [Pauses briefly] *It does connect to chimpanzees, I assure you. What I'm suggesting is that, while Peter Benchley may have inadvertently demonized sharks, his underlying emphasis was correct. Horror is a genre that functions as a safeguard—it prompts our species to confront existential threats, real or imagined. If Benchley had written about chimpanzees rather than sharks, I believe the narrative could have yielded even more significant societal benefit.*

Eerie Ebenezer: [Frowning] *How do you mean "greater societal benefit"?*

Bryan Harrison: *.Allow me to clarify. While sharks are undeniably formidable creatures, they pale in comparison to the behavioral complexities—and dangers—presented by chimpanzees. The public perception of chimpanzees has long been skewed by media portrayals that present them as benign, diaper-clad performers, amusing and harmless. This could not be further from the truth. Chimpanzees engage in cannibalism. They have been documented consuming their own offspring as well as the infants of gorillas. These acts are not driven purely by hunger but appear to satisfy...dare I say...some darker impulse. Moreover, chimpanzees have dismembered human beings—ripping out eyes and tearing off lips, fingers, and genitals. When they taste blood, they enter a state of frenzied aggression, drumming their chests in what can only be described as a macabre display of dominance and power.*

Eerie Ebenezer: [Incredulous] *And you've seen this with your own eyes?*

Bryan Harrison: [Visibly uncomfortable, yet maintaining a formal tone] *Yes. My academic career necessitates a certain degree of clinical detachment. I am compelled to present chimpanzees as a species worthy of protection, vital to the biodiversity of their ecosystems. However, having personally witnessed their violent behavior, I find myself in an internal conflict. This species—despite its biological significance—is, in moments of aggression, nothing short of monstrous.*

Eerie Ebenezer: [Carefully] *That's a strong word to use—monstrous—as in...*

Bryan Harrison: [Nods slowly] *As in monster. And I do not use it lightly. Some in psychology believe humanity's concept of the "boogeyman" originated from interactions with creatures such as these. The problem, Eerie, lies in juxtaposing my empirical observations with the prevailing narrative. My colleagues and I are expected to advocate for the protection of these animals, and indeed, from a conservation standpoint, that remains crucial. But the darker truth—that these creatures possess the capacity for extraordinary violence—goes largely unacknowledged. I have seen them rip apart colleagues. I have seen their methodical brutality in action, not as isolated incidents but as a pattern of behavior that challenges our anthropocentric assumptions about our place in the natural order.*

Eerie Ebenezer: [Pauses] *So, the scientific community won't admit how dangerous they really are?*

Bryan Harrison: [Eyes filled with emotion, but voice steady] *In the interest of conservation and maintaining funding streams for research, no. It's considered counterproductive to highlight these more terrifying aspects of chimpanzee behavior. Yet, as someone who has seen the carnage firsthand, I feel it is imperative that the public understand the truth. We are conditioned to fear sharks, bears, or wolves, but the real danger may come from species we've been led to believe are gentle or intellectually akin to ourselves.*

Eerie Ebenezer: [Slightly unnerved] *And that's why you're here today? To speak a truth that's too dangerous for the scientific community to admit?*

Bryan Harrison: [Exhales deeply, wiping his eyes] *Precisely. I came here because people need to understand—these animals, these so-called 'gentle apes'—are capable of atrocities that we've barely scratched the surface of in popular discourse. They aren't just tools for understanding our evolutionary past. They are a threat that we've dangerously underestimated.*

CHAPTER 18

Eb stood before the impaled Sasquatch. The monster's massive body slumped in the pitfall they'd constructed in Savage River State Forest. Blood soaked the fur. Eb's eyes scanned the monster for any signs of life. Eb climbed down the rope that Dirty Chap had dropped down for Doc. Then Dirty Chap climbed down with Cora following behind.

"Yo, dawg," Dirty Chap said, his voice echoing in the tight space. He stood beside the creature, shaking his head slowly. "This thing's big, for real, for real."

"That's what I said," Cora added, her eyes focused on the creature's body, but her voice wavered slightly. She stood straighter than usual, trying to mask her exhaustion and guilt. "The size is impressive, but we need to stay focused."

Eb frowned, sensing Cora's strain. "Fall back," he ordered, sharper than usual. His tone reflected his own mounting tension.

Dirty Chap and Cora took a few steps back as Eb descended into the pit. He stood over the Sasquatch, its twisted face frozen in a snarl. Drawing his Bowie knife, he moved with swift, almost automatic motions. *Schwack!* One cut. Then another—until the head rolled free from the body.

"C'mon, dawg," Dirty Chap said, his voice lower, more somber than before. "This ain't *Blade*, man. We're not hunting vampires."

Eb wiped his blade clean, staring down at the decapitated head, the sharp teeth still glistening with blood. "Our ancestors would've called it a monster," he said quietly, avoiding eye contact. "And right now, I'm not gonna argue with them."

He dropped the head, wiping his hands on his already bloodstained shirt. But the sight didn't leave him. Something felt off, wrong even, about what he'd just done.

"You've changed," Cora said, her voice more direct than before. She wasn't accusing, just observing. "This used to be your obsession—something you cared about more than anything."

Eb met her eyes briefly before turning away. "Yeah, well," he said, muttering, "that was before I saw Muleskinner's throat caved in."

Cora flinched, the mention of Muleskinner dragging more guilt to the surface. She hadn't even had time to process his death, and now she was standing over another kill. She blinked rapidly, trying to push it aside.

Dirty Chap knelt by the body, pointing to the scars along the creature's chest and face. "Yo, check this out. This one's bigger than the others we hit. Faster too. Look at these cuts—it's a straight-up warrior."

Eb didn't respond immediately, feeling the blood still rushing through his veins. The violence, the necessity of it—it all felt too easy now. Too automatic.

Cora stepped closer, her voice steady but with a slight tremor. "What he's suggesting is that this is the Alpha. The leader."

"The Alpha?" Eb asked, his skepticism cutting through his doubts for a moment.

"Look at the evidence," Cora said, gesturing toward the creature's scars. "This one's larger, battle-hardened. It dominated the others. You've studied pack dynamics in other species. You know this fits."

Eb took a deep breath, his mind racing. Memories of his interviews with Dr. Bryan Harrison and Dr. Danny Vendramdt flickered in his mind. The term "Alpha" echoed, but something still felt... off. This kill—it wasn't sitting right with him.

"I don't know," Eb said quietly. His mind lingered on Muleskinner, on the blood that seemed to stick to him no matter how much he wiped it off. What if this wasn't the Alpha? What if they were wrong?

Cora's face softened, but her voice stayed firm. "We've taken down what seems to be the dominant one. We need to keep moving, Eb. We can end this before anyone else gets hurt."

He looked at her, seeing the cracks in her resolve, the weight of Muleskinner's death still hanging over her, but she kept pushing forward. Cora's determination was clear, even as guilt gnawed at her.

Dirty Chap stood, brushing dirt off his hands. "Yo, I get it, man. This ain't easy. But we gotta keep moving, or we're next."

Eb nodded slowly. "Yeah," he said, more to himself than anyone else. "That could be."

As the team regrouped, he noticed something different about Dirty Chap. He wasn't cracking jokes like usual. He looked serious, more than Eb had seen him before.

"Chap," Eb said quietly, "you good?"

Dirty Chap took a deep breath, glancing at the dead Sasquatch. "Yeah, I'm good," he said, but there was a pause. He rubbed the back of his neck, as if weighing something in his mind. "I just... This thing, man. It ain't what I signed up for, you know? I mean, we're supposed to protect people, but... no one ever mentioned monsters."

Eb looked at him, really looked at him for the first time since the mission started. Dirty Chap wasn't just the tough guy. There was fear there—real fear. "Yeah," Eb said softly. "None of us signed up for this."

Dirty Chap nodded, his eyes lingering on the creature. "We gotta stay alive, dawg. For Muleskinner. For all of us."

Eb felt his chest tighten. Now, he was listening. Dirty Chap wasn't making excuses, he never had been. His words weren't just in this for survival. It was about something more—keeping each other alive—keeping his friends alive.

Eb took a step back, viewing not just the creature but Cora and Dirty Chap.

And as he glanced at Cora, still standing strong despite the weight on her shoulders, he realized something else: he was becoming the one they were all looking to.

He didn't feel ready. Truth be told, he didn't want it. But Muleskinner's bloodied helmet still rested on his head.

"We gotta move," Eb said, his voice steadying. "We've got more out there."

Without another word, he climbed the ladder, the doubts still clinging to him. But something inside him shifted. He wasn't just following anymore.

And maybe... just maybe... he was starting to lead.

Interview with Dr. Bryan Harrison and Dr. Mark, aired on *WMSC Maryland News*.
[Audio Transcript]

[SFX: Soft static, studio ambiance, faint rustling of papers]

News Anchor: *Good evening, Maryland. Tonight, we bring you a special segment on the recent tragedy—the encounter with a Maryland-based private security firm inside the Savage River State Forest that resulted in catastrophic outcomes. Joining us tonight are two distinguished experts: Dr. Bryan Harrison, a leading primatologist from Goucher University, and Dr. Mark, a noted expert in Neanderthal studies. Thank you both for being here.*

Dr. Bryan Harrison: *Thank you for having us. It is essential to address these matters [pauses, regaining emotional composure].*

Dr. Mark: *It's unfortunate that we have to be here. Bryan here has cut up so many frogs in labs, so it's probably weird to see a scientist so emotional...but the reality was that...Eb was our mate.*

News Anchor: *With all respect to the victims and their families, let's dive right into it. From the information gathered, we understand that Eerie Ebenezer Edwards, whom you just referred to as a "mate" or "friend" for our North American audience, the interim leader of the team, sensed something was wrong before things took a turn for the worse. Dr. Harrison, could you explain where the breakdown occurred in their understanding of the situation?*

Dr. Bryan Harrison: *Certainly. What we are dealing with here is a fundamental misjudgment of the species' behavior and the broader ecological context in which these events took place. Mr. Edwards, while not a formally trained scientist, possessed a remarkable intuition, something field researchers often develop over time. His sense that something was awry stemmed from subtle cues in the environment—cues his team either dismissed or misinterpreted.*

[There's a brief pause as the anchor waits, sensing more to come.]

Dr. Bryan Harrison: *Tragically, that instinct, while sharp, wasn't acted upon swiftly enough.*

News Anchor: *When you say instinct, what exactly was Mr. Edwards picking up on?*

[There's a moment of silence as the gravity of the question sinks in.]

Dr. Mark: *Ah, well, ol' Eerie had seen a lot by that point. He wasn't just a bloke with a gun; he was a thinker. They thought they'd killed the Alpha—big mistake. When you've been out there long enough, you start to feel when somethin' ain't right, even if you can't put it into words. Eerie knew it in his bones.*

Dr. Bryan Harrison: *Correct, Yes, precisely. The key issue here is one of misidentification. The creature they killed, while formidable, was not a leader, nor was it operating in a way indicative of an Alpha. Its behavior was far too erratic, suggestive not of territorial defense but of desperation.*

News Anchor: *Desperation? So they mistook it for an Alpha when it wasn't?*

Dr. Mark: *Spot on. The poor bugger they took down wasn't the top dog. It was desperate, likely driven out from its group. A loner. Eerie saw it straight away, but by then, the damage was done.*

News Anchor: *So Ebenezer's instincts told him something was wrong, but he couldn't convince the team?*

Dr. Bryan Harrison: *Exactly. This is a well-documented issue in fieldwork, where individuals may trust empirical evidence over instinct or intuition, even when the latter is more accurate in the immediate context. While Eerie's team may have felt a sense of accomplishment, believing they had neutralized the greatest threat, they were operating under a false sense of security. They failed to understand the broader social dynamics of the Sasquatch species—a species that remains largely uncharted in terms of its social hierarchy and behavioral ecology.*

News Anchor: *And this miscalculation led to the... incident that followed?*

[Another pause]

Dr. Bryan Harrison: *Indeed. Based on the available evidence, the Sasquatch they encountered was a solitary creature, most likely an outcast. In primate species, including the great apes, outcasts behave differently from group leaders or Alphas. They are driven by base survival instincts, often acting unpredictably. What the team faced after that encounter, I suspect, was the true Alpha. The ensuing events—while we cannot say for certain without a full debrief—suggest that the Alpha acted with the precision and strategy we observe in apex predators.*

News Anchor: *Could you elaborate on that? What made this encounter so unique compared to other primate behavior?*

Dr. Mark: *Well, there's this tendency to compare Sasquatch to other great apes, yeah? Gorillas, orangutans, you name it. But the thing is, you can't lump them all together. Sasquatch is its own species. Its own bloody category. It doesn't follow the same rules. Most folks want to either turn 'em into some fairy tale creature, like a troll, or they wanna slot 'em in with apes they already know. But Sasquatch... Sasquatch is Sasquatch. And that's where the team went wrong.*

Dr. Bryan Harrison: *Precisely. The behavioral patterns of the Sasquatch or now its scientific name, Dryopithecus, while sharing some superficial similarities with known primates, are distinct. What we've come to understand, albeit still in its infancy, is that the Sasquatch displays a level of strategic intelligence not typically associated with other great apes. Its actions are not reactionary, but calculated, deliberate. And that makes it far more dangerous than the team realized at the time.*

News Anchor: *So, to summarize—Eerie Ebenezer's team believed they had eliminated the Alpha, but they were tragically mistaken?*

Dr. Bryan Harrison: *Yes. The aforementioned creature was not an alpha predator but a troop pariah driven into the pitfall not by dominance...but desperation. They believed the threat had been neutralized when, in fact, the most dangerous creature was still out there, observing, waiting. Eerie sensed this intuitively, but as Dr. Mark said, they'd already acted. The real Alpha, with its superior strategic capabilities, would not have acted out of emotion, but rather with a singular goal in mind: to eradicate the intruders from its territory. This kind of response is consistent with apex predator behavior across numerous species, and we believe it was no different here.*

News Anchor: *And the aftermath...?*

[Both scientists fall silent]

Dr. Mark: *Let's just say... Eerie knew somethin' was wrong. He always knew. And by the time it all unraveled, well, let's just say the cost was far too high.*

News Anchor: *But for the record, can you say definitively what happened next?*

Dr. Bryan Harrison: *Without complete data, it is difficult to state definitively. However, based on the patterns of behavior observed in similar apex species, it is likely that the Alpha responded with calculated aggression. While the details of what happened after that are not fully available, it is safe to say that the consequences were... tragic.*

CHAPTER 19

The team pressed deeper into Savage River State Forest. The wind howled through the trees. Eb kept his eyes trained on the faint footprints. His heart thudded against his chest—pounding more from the tension than the exertion. He felt the weight of leadership heavy on his shoulders—*Was this really my call to make?*

"I can still see it," Eb said, keeping his voice steady.

Dirty Chap jogged up beside him, slapping him on the back. "Top dawg, huh? You got us movin', for real."

Eb forced a smile, but inside, uncertainty gnawed at him. *I wish I felt as sure as he does.* Dirty Chap jogged back to his position, his grin doing little to calm Eb's doubts.

Doc, his boots squelching in the softening earth, caught up to Eb. "You see that?" he asked, pointing skyward, his brow furrowed.

"The sign?" Eb asked, still focused on the ground.

"No, man—up there," Doc said, more insistent.

Eb finally looked up, noticing the storm clouds swirling overhead. The wind carried a chill that made him shiver.

"Storm's coming," Doc muttered, his knee tapping restlessly. "I can feel it."

"Trust your gut," Eb said under his breath, lost in his own head.

Doc leaned in. "What?"

"I said, yeah, it looks like rain," Eb repeated louder.

Doc shook his head. "This isn't just rain, Eb. It's gonna be a storm—a big one. Mathematically speaking, the odds of us getting through this unscathed are dropping fast."

Eb's stomach churned. "Turning back is probably the smart move."

Doc's shoulders relaxed for a moment, but Eb wasn't finished.

"But ethically, Doc, we can't leave her."

Doc groaned, his irritation rising. "C'mon, man. We didn't sign up to walk into a storm like this! You're not even the leader—you know this isn't your call."

Eb's jaw clenched. He knew Doc was right in some ways, but responsibility pulled him in another direction. "Dahlia's still out there, Doc. We're not leaving her behind."

Doc crossed his arms. "You think duty's gonna keep us dry when that storm hits? You know this kind of thinking gets people killed."

Eb's mouth opened, but no words came out. Doc had a point, and part of him knew it. But something deeper—something tied to Dahlia, to Muleskinner, to Cora—pushed him forward.

"Do what you want," Doc said, throwing his hands up in frustration. "But when that sky opens up, and we're waist-deep in trouble, don't say I didn't warn you."

Before Eb could reply, Cora's voice cut through the rising wind. "Hey, come check this out."

They hurried to where Cora stood, her arms folded across her chest. She stood beside a massive rock, half-buried in the ground, its surface jagged and scarred with deep cuts.

Dirty Chap came up next, glancing between the rock and the nearby riverbank. "Yo, this thing? Nah, man, it prolly drifted up here. River's been wild lately, tossin' stuff like a blender."

Cora raised an eyebrow. "A river did this? Seriously, Chap?"

Dirty Chap shrugged. "I mean, rivers'll throw anything if it's got the time."

Doc knelt beside the rock, running his fingers along the edges. "These cuts are too deliberate. This wasn't rolled around."

A chill crawled up Eb's spine. Something about the rock felt wrong—out of place.

"This didn't wash up," Eb muttered, his eyes locked on the rock. "It was thrown."

The wind picked up again, and the first few drops of rain began to fall, dotting the ground around them.

CHAPTER 20

The downpour was relentless, turning the forest floor into thick mud. Eb yanked his poncho tighter around him, but the water still soaked through, chilling him to the bone. Each step was a slog, and the silence between him and the team was as heavy as the storm clouds above them.

Doc was right, Eb thought, the weight of his earlier decisions pressing down on him harder than the rain. He didn't need to look back to know Doc was glaring at him.

Eb signaled for the team to halt, dropping to one knee and pulling out a poncho from his assault pack. The tension in the air between him and Cora felt thicker than the rain around them.

"You got one?" he asked, his voice low but purposeful.

Cora knelt beside him, pulling her own poncho out. The rain plastered her hair to her face, but there was something fierce about the way she moved—steady, focused. Her determination was as sharp as the storm bearing down on them.

"Sexy," Eb murmured, half-joking, half-admiring her resilience.

Cora rolled her eyes, a smirk tugging at her lips. "You wish," she shot back, but there was a hint of warmth in her voice. She didn't pull away from him this time—maybe she didn't want to.

Their shared look was brief, but it said enough. There was something between them now, something deeper than flirtation. But neither of them had time to explore it. Not now.

Eb stood, signaling for the group to move forward. The rain fell in heavy sheets, turning the once-clear trail into a slippery mess. The only sound was the steady drum of water hitting the earth, drowning out the usual forest noises.

Dirty Chap trudged beside him, his usual swagger dampened by the storm. "Yo, man, this... this don't feel right."

Eb glanced over at him, hearing the vulnerability in his voice. Dirty Chap, the guy who was always joking, always confident, was starting to crack.

"We'll be fine," Eb said, but the words felt hollow even to him.

Behind them, Accidental's voice cut through the rain. "Statistically speaking, our odds of keeping pace in this terrain are dropping fast. But if we stop now, we're looking at a zero percent chance of finding her. Keep pushing."

Dirty Chap chuckled darkly. "Man, you and your numbers. Just tell me the odds of us not getting killed."

Eb watched the engineer; Accidental didn't respond, his eyes scanning the landscape as he kept calculating.

Eb pushed forward, his boots sinking into the mud with each step. The rain made everything harder—tracking, moving, thinking. The cold seeped into his bones, making him feel like the forest was closing in around them.

Great apes hate water, he reminded himself, trying to stay focused. *If the Sasquatch are anything like other great apes, they'll be seeking shelter.*

But the rain wouldn't let up. The downpour felt like it was coming from all directions, drumming against his poncho and the earth beneath his feet.

A branch snapped somewhere in the distance, barely audible over the roar of the rain. Eb froze, his heart pounding in his chest. His eyes darted toward the sound, but nothing moved.

"This rain'll stop a great ape in its tracks," Eb said aloud, his voice tense. But as he stood there, listening to the storm, he wondered if that were true.

CHAPTER 21

Rain beat against the Savage River State Forest in solid, heavy sheets. The deluge drenched them, covering them in a terrible combination of moisture and misery, but still, the team trudged forward.

"Yuck," Eb muttered.

With each step, his boots sank deeper into the thickening mud, the ground sucking at their soles. The downpour swallowed the usual sounds of the woods, replacing the music of the forest with the relentless drumming of water and the occasional crack of a branch overhead. The world around them seemed to hold its breath, as if waiting.

Eb squinted through the curtain of rain. A dark shape loomed ahead, half-hidden by the storm. His hand shot up, signaling the group to stop.

Dirty Chap jogged forward, his swagger faltering as he glanced around the drenched trees. "Yo, what we lookin' at up here?" Dirty Chap asked. "Bigfoot leave us a lil' somethin' special?"

"What is that?" Eb asked as they stepped closer.

As they approached, the shape resolved into a massive black bear. The creature lay sprawled grotesquely on the forest floor—its death unmistakable.

"Yummy," Eb muttered.

Claw marks carved deep into the dead bear's fur-covered flesh. Its limbs twisted at impossible angles, as if flung aside with effortless strength.

"Man..." Dirty Chap knelt beside the carcass, his eyes widening. "That's messed up, dawg. For real. A bear? Like... what could even do this?"

"There's a whole troop of them," Eb said. "They must have torn at it."

The bear's blood oozed into the mud, swirling with the rain in thick, sluggish streams. Its throat gaped open, not just torn but ravaged—flesh hanging in ragged, wet shreds. Tendons stretched and snapped like strands of frayed rope. Dark muscle glistened beneath the gash, still twitching as if the body hadn't entirely let go.

Its chest had been split apart, ribs cracked and splayed outward, jutting like broken ivory. Its internal organs spilled free, slick and swollen, glistening under the relentless rain. The intestines sprawled across the earth, bile-streaked and twitching in the downpour. The heart, half-ripped from its arteries, dangled limply by thin, bloodied threads, barely clinging to the ruined body.

Doc crouched beside the mutilated animal, his fingers tracing the ragged edges of the wound. "Nothing in these woods has the power to do this. Not wolves, not another bear... not even a person."

Cora stood back, her sharp gaze sweeping the treeline. She didn't flinch, her jaw tight. "Do predators just leave food out like this?"

Eb stepped closer, his stomach twisting at the sight. The bear had been strong, fast. The picture formed slowly, grimly, in his mind, each piece snapping into place like a puzzle he wished he could ignore.

"That ain't food," Eb muttered, his words nearly drowned by the rain. His eyes flicked toward the trees, scanning the dense underbrush. "It's a message."

Dirty Chap shifted uneasily, his bravado slipping. "Nah, man, that's some wild movie sh—uh, stuff right there. Y'all feelin' this?"

The forest, vast and indifferent moments before, seemed to shrink around them, its shadows bending and stretching, twisting with the movement of the trees. Shadows shaped like dark fingers crept forward—long and reaching—as if the woods themselves watched from every corner.

Eb watched as Dirty Chap's eyes darted between the trees, his cocky stance dissolving into raw unease. "Yo, man, I dunno about this. We gotta keep movin'. Like, right now. These woods got eyes, bro. Straight up."

Eb fought for breath—his lungs heavy with the weight of realization:

It's a threat.

Eerie Ebenezer Paranormal Podcast

Special Guest Danny Vendramdt, Author of *Them Against Us: How We Defeated The Neanderthals*

[Interview taken prior to the events in Savage River Forest State Park]

Eerie Ebenezer: *We're back, still here with Danny Vendramdt, author of* Them Against Us. *Danny, before we move forward, I want to circle back to something you mentioned earlier—the Great Emu War. It caught me off guard. You're talking about Neanderthals, but then you bring up... emus?*

Danny Vendramdt: *[laughs] Yeah, mate, I reckon that threw a spanner in the works. But, I tell ya, it ties in. People hear "Emu War" and reckon it's a bit of a joke. But, nah, there's more to it than meets the eye.*

Eerie Ebenezer: *Right, I mean, it's kind of hard to wrap my head around. Your countrymen—no offense—were defeated by a bunch of big birds. And what does that have to do with Neanderthals?*

Danny Vendramdt: *No worries, mate, none taken. Us Aussies, we've got thick skin. The thing is, the Emu War was about more than just a few blokes havin' a go at a bunch of birds. It's about how we think we can control nature. Just like with the Neanderthals, we thought we had the upper hand, but nature's always got a few tricks up its sleeve, doesn't it?*

Eerie Ebenezer: *Okay, explain that. How does the Great Emu War fit into this?*

Danny Vendramdt: *Righto. Let me take ya back. It's the 1930s, right? Farmers out in the sticks, mostly blokes who fought in World War I, are tryin' to scrape a living off the land. The government gave 'em some land, but didn't give 'em much else. Then, bang, you've got thousands of bloody emus rockin' up to their paddocks, rippin' their crops to shreds.*

Eerie Ebenezer: *And then Major Meredith comes in with the big guns.*

Danny Vendramdt: *Exactly. Major G.P.W. Meredith—a top bloke, smart as a whip. He's artillery, right? The kind of fella who can fire off a shell from miles away and hit the target every time. But here's where it gets tricky. Meredith's job was to outsmart the emus, but those birds weren't playin' ball. They were organized, mate, like a footy team. Fast as lightning, darting about, and they were bloody clever. Meredith could've hit a target a hundred times, but the emus just kept dodgin' the bullets.*

Eerie Ebenezer: *So they're not just birds?*

Danny Vendramdt: *Nah, mate, they were something else. Meredith and his boys were ready to fight a proper war, but this wasn't like chargin' trenches. The emus, they weren't thinkin' like men—they were thinkin' like animals. Fast, elusive, and communicatin' in ways we didn't understand. Meredith was fightin' a losing battle from the get-go, because he was using human logic on a problem that was all nature.*

Eerie Ebenezer: *Okay, but Major Meredith was still... defeated by birds.*

Danny Vendramdt: *Too right! He was beaten, and not because he wasn't smart. It's 'cause he didn't understand the beast he was up against. The emus, mate, they were built for survival. Meredith's lot had guns and smarts, but the birds had instincts. It wasn't just about firepower. It was about the fact that we underestimated them. Thought we could control 'em, but they ran circles around us.*

Eerie Ebenezer: *So what was the fallout from all of this? The way you're talking, it wasn't just a joke.*

Danny Vendramdt: *Nah, mate. Here's the rub: while the military's gettin' made fun of, the farmers out there were sufferin'. These blokes came back from the war thinkin' they were gonna build a life, and now their crops are stuffed because of the emus. The wheat was wrecked, they couldn't feed their families. It was dire, mate. You talk about the Great Depression? This made it worse. The blokes couldn't even make enough to put tucker on the table. Some of 'em didn't make it. Suicides weren't uncommon. You'd have proud men, veterans, lookin' out at their destroyed fields and thinkin' they had nothin' left.*

Eerie Ebenezer: *So the real cost wasn't just losing crops?*

Danny Vendramdt: *Exactly. People died, mate. Not from gunfire, but from despair. When the land goes belly up, so do the people. Kids went hungry, blokes went to the pub one last time, and then they were done. It was tragic, and it all started because a bunch of birds couldn't be controlled.*

Eerie Ebenezer: *Wow. That's much darker than I expected. What's the connection here with Neanderthals, though?*

Danny Vendramdt: *Same story, mate. We thought we were smarter than the Neanderthals. Thought we'd just sweep 'em away with our fancy tools and our bigger brains. But that's where we got it wrong. Like with the emus, we underestimated them. The Neanderthals had their own ways—survival instincts, communication, things we still don't understand. We won in the end, but not 'cause we were smarter. We were just more relentless. The emus? They showed us what happens when we think we've got nature all figured out.*

Eerie Ebenezer: *So we're making the same mistakes over and over?*

Danny Vendramdt: *Exactly. It's a reminder, mate. Whether it's emus, Neanderthals, or whatever. The minute we get cocky, nature's ready to knock us down a peg.*

CHAPTER 22

The rain had let up. The deluge had left the Savage River State Forest wet and steaming.

"Make sure you're drinking water," Eb said, knowing the impending humidity would be unbearable.

Two, maybe three hours had passed since the worst of it. The team had stowed their ponchos and continued in the search for Dahlia Rhodes. The sound of boots sinking into the soaked ground was the only thing breaking the eerie, suffocating silence. The air about them grew not only with humidity but a palpable feeling of unease.

"My gut is screaming," Eb said to himself.

But while his gut screamed—a human life—that of Dahlia Rhodes somewhere out in this nightmare—drove him forward.

Eb's eyes studied the muddy foot sign above. He felt rigid as every muscle in his body coiled tight. The rain might've stopped, but something else had started. His skin prickled with tension and that familiar churn of dread bubbled in his gut.

The heavy rainfall had beaten down the canopy. Now, a dull light shown through casting the world in a shade of gray. Eb adjusted his grip on the carbine, his eyes narrowing as he scanned the shifting shadows.

"Yo, I swear," Dirty Chap said, "this place is givin' me the creeps."

Eb didn't respond. Something flickered. The movement was ahead. Not necessarily on the ground, but a change in color—a shadow flashed across the mud-soaked surface.

Eb raised his weapon, aiming toward the canopy above. The others followed suit—weapons ready—scanning the trees above.

"What is it?" Cora whispered, stepping up beside him, her voice tight.

"You know what it is," Eb said and he scanned the treeline.

The monster had returned.

Eb continued his scan of the sky above. Shadows between the trees stretched and twisted with the fading light.

And then he heard it. Faint, but unmistakable—*crack*—something heavy stepping on a branch. Eb's heart beat against his chest with hummingbird-like rhythm. His eyes snapped to Cora.

"They're here," she whispered.

Another sound followed, closer now—a low, rumbling growl that rolled through the underbrush. Before anyone could react, a sharp whizzing sound sliced through the air. A rock slammed into the ground, inches from Cora.

Eb returned fire—*BANG BANG BANG BANG!*

The branches and leaves danced, as if the Sasquatch traveled among them in near invisibility.

Another rock came flying from the treeline, striking Cora in the shoulder. She grunted, collapsing to one knee, clutching her arm.

Indignance gripped Eb, he fired his weapon—*BANG BANG BANG!*

"Save your ammunition!" Dirty Chap yelled and waved his hands. "Save it!"

Cora grimaced, her face pale, but her eyes sharp. "I'm fine," she managed through gritted teeth, pulling herself behind cover.

Eb's eyes darted through the trees, catching glimpses of movement—large, fast, and silent. His carbine snapped up, but he couldn't lock onto anything solid.

The forest echoed as the Sasquatch filled the scene with its hate-filled pant-hoots.

Shadows flitted between the trees—too quick to follow. Another rock whistled past, smacking into the mud with a wet thud.

"They're moving in!" Doc called from behind a tree, already lining up his shot.

And then it came. A roar ripped through the air, and something massive crashed through the underbrush. A Sasquatch, bigger than any they'd seen before, barreled toward them. It rushed in a gorilla-like motion—rampaging forward in a quadrupedal rush.

"Fire!" Eb shouted, his finger squeezing the trigger as the creature came into view. Gunfire erupted in the clearing, bullets tearing through the damp air, but the Sasquatch barely flinched.

It closed the distance in seconds, slamming into Doc with bone-crunching force. Doc flew backward, his body hitting the mud hard, skidding near a fallen log.

"Doc!" Cora half-rose to go to him, but another rock slammed into the tree beside her, forcing her back down.

"We got more incoming!" Dirty Chap yelled, spraying bullets into the trees. Eb followed his line of sight and saw them—two more Sasquatches, moving fast, impossibly fast for their size.

Eb fired, catching one of the creatures in the side. It howled, stumbling, but kept coming. The second one crouched low, muscles bunching before it charged straight at them with a snarl.

"They're too fast!" Cora yelled, trying to line up a shot, her injured shoulder hanging uselessly.

"Focus fire!" Eb ordered, directing the team's fire at the closest creature.

The first Sasquatch collapsed in a hail of bullets, its massive body crashing into the mud with a guttural roar. The second, bleeding from several wounds, hesitated—its baleful red eyes flicking between them—before darting back into the shadows.

Eb lowered his carbine, his chest heaving, breath coming in ragged bursts. The forest fell silent again, like the creatures had never been there at all.

Doc groaned from where he lay, clutching his side, blood staining the mud beneath him. "They're playing with us," he muttered weakly, struggling to sit up.

Cora's jaw clenched; her eyes fierce despite the pain etched across her face. "We need to get out of here. Doc's hurt. We can't push forward like this."

Eb scanned the treeline again, the heavy silence pressing in on them. "We're not staying here. We move, now. But we're going back."

"Man, we can't go back," Dirty Chap said. "You saw 'em—they ain't gonna let us leave."

Eb's eyes hardened. "We don't have a choice. Cora's hurt, Doc's banged up... we can't keep going like this."

Reluctantly, the team began to retreat, moving cautiously through the thick mud. The earlier rain had turned the forest into a trap of slick earth and swollen streams, slowing their pace. The sky darkened further as they pushed on, the light bleeding away until the forest became a sea of grey shadows.

"Fine then," Dirty Chap said. "How do we get back?"

Eb's jaw tightened. He scanned the area. The whole area looked the same.

He knew the truth: The storm, the attack—it had thrown them off course.

Cora limped beside him, her breath coming in short, sharp bursts, but her gaze steady. "No... no, Eb, we're not lost, are we?"

Eb didn't answer. The truth churned in his gut: They were lost.

CHAPTER 23

Eb knelt beside Cora, her back propped against the base of a Tulip Poplar. She grimaced, pressing her hand to the injured shoulder, blood seeping through her fingers.

"Man, you're tough," Eb said, voice low as he inspected the wound. Her skin felt hot beneath his fingers, slick with blood, and despite the shallow, pain-filled gasps she took, Cora managed to tighten her mouth into something like a smile. But her raven-colored eyes told the truth—pain, deep and relentless.

"I'm fine," she said, but the tremor in her voice betrayed her.

Eb's stomach churned, a dark coldness settling over him. His hand lingered on hers, both for her comfort and his own. There wasn't time to say what he wanted—what needed to be said. Maybe there never would be.

The truth gnawed at him: we're lost. The storm, the ambush, the whole Savage River State Forest—it had swallowed them whole. Dahlia was out there somewhere, but she might as well have been on another planet. Now, with Cora hurt, Doc barely hanging on, and the Sasquatch stalking them, it felt like the nightmare was closing in.

Doc groaned a few feet away, his hand pressed tight to his side, blood pooling beneath him and soaking into the mud. He trembled as he tried to shift, his breath rattling in short, shallow gasps.

"Yo, Eb, we can't just sit here. Those things are out there—watchin' us, waitin'. We gotta get outta here, man. Now," Dirty Chap muttered, pacing with growing agitation.

Eb's eyes darted to the shadows stretching between the trees. They flickered ominously in the dying light, as if the forest itself was alive, closing in. Worse yet, they were so far off course that everything looked unfamiliar, alien. The forest had become a trap.

"We can't move," Eb finally said, his voice tight. "Not yet. We need shelter."

"Shelter?" Dirty Chap spat, throwing his hands up. "Man, we don't got time for no freakin' treehouse! We got freaks out there waitin' to tear us apart! We're sittin' ducks!"

"Aye, we need to hunker down and build a fighting hole ASAP," Accidental cut in, his voice calm but urgent. "We'll rig somethin' up—pitfall, makeshift camo. It ain't much, but it'll slow those freaks down."

Eb nodded sharply. "Do it. Dirty, help him."

Dirty Chap opened his mouth to argue, but one look at Eb, and he snapped his jaw shut. "Fine," he grumbled, though his bravado had slipped. "Let's get this done."

"Chap, grab the 550 cord and that log over there. We're setting a trip pit," Accidental barked, already working fast. He dug into the soft ground with a makeshift e-tool, shoveling dirt and mud aside as quickly as his hands would allow. Dirty Chap grunted as he hoisted a heavy log over his shoulder, slinging the rappel rope around it to secure it in place above the pit.

"Man, this thing's heavy," Dirty Chap said through gritted teeth, his arms flexing as he heaved the log into position.

Accidental didn't pause. "Keep it steady, mate. We need that to trigger just right. If they fall into this pit, it'll be our only chance to take 'em down. Set those punji sticks up tight. Fast."

The two men worked frantically, pulling branches, securing the logs, digging into the thick, wet earth. The pit was crude, but it would be deadly. The sharpened stakes were hidden under a thin layer of leaves and mud, ready to impale whatever fell in.

While the others worked, Eb turned back to Cora. The weight of everything pressed down on him—Cora's injuries, the dark, steaming forest, the ever-present sense of dread hanging in the air. The scent of mud and blood clung to his nostrils, suffocating him.

"Stay still," he whispered, his hand still resting on hers. "Let them handle it. You need to rest."

"I'm fine, Eb," she whispered back, though her voice was strained, too soft, too weak.

Their eyes locked, and in that moment, he saw more than just the pain. He saw her strength, her resilience—everything that made her irreplaceable.

"We'll find her," she said, but Eb heard the doubt in her voice. She meant Dahlia, but the way she said it made it sound like she was losing hope.

I can't lose you too, Eb thought. *I won't.*

Accidental and Dirty Chap grunted as they finished the pitfall trap, the sound of snapping branches and sloshing mud echoing around them. Logs were hoisted into place, covered by leaves and dirt, masking the deadly trap beneath.

"How long?" Eb called out, his eyes flicking nervously toward the trees. The forest had grown darker, every rustle of leaves like the prelude to an attack.

"Five mikes, tops!" Accidental barked, yanking the cord tight. "This ain't a FOB, but it'll slow those hairy bastards down."

The pitfall was ready, but Eb's gut twisted. They were buying time—time they didn't have.

Doc groaned again, louder this time, his hand slipping from his wound as blood streamed down his side. His eyes fluttered as he cursed under his breath.

"Maron, I ain't walkin' outta here, am I?" Doc muttered, his thick Baltimore accent slurring the words. "Freakin' cannolis, I shoulda stayed home."

Cora's eyes widened. "Doc—" she started, but her face twisted in pain, her shoulder slumping.

"Hold on," Eb whispered, brushing a strand of hair from her face. His heart squeezed painfully in his chest. *God, don't let this be it.* He couldn't lose Cora—not like this, not here. Not now.

The forest closed in around them, the shadows darker, the air heavier.

"They're playin' us," Doc murmured, his voice thick with the Baltimore drawl that became more pronounced with each word. "These things... they're messin' with us."

Accidental glanced up from the pitfall, his face slick with mud and sweat. "We gotta move, Eb. This ain't gonna hold them for long."

Eb's heart raced. Cora's breath hitched, her strength fading fast. Doc was barely conscious, and every second they spent here made them more vulnerable. The pitfall would slow the Sasquatch, but it wouldn't stop them.

"We're not gonna make it, are we?" Cora whispered, her voice so soft, so full of fear.

Eb clenched his jaw, the words heavy on his tongue. He looked into her eyes, his voice rough with determination.

"Yeah," he said, brushing his thumb over her cheek. "We will."

But deep down, he knew he was lying.

Interview with Dr. Bryan Harrison and Dr. Mark, aired on WMSC Maryland News.
[Audio Transcript]

[SFX: Soft static, studio ambiance, faint rustling of papers]

Reporter: *So, the burning question on everyone's mind... why would a Sasquatch kidnap a woman like Dahlia Rhodes?*

[SFX: Pause, the faint shift of papers, soft ambient silence]

Dr. Danny Vendramdt: *Y'know, that's the question people laugh at, but there's history here. Great apes kidnapping humans is not unheard of. Have you heard of the tragedy of Harambe? Or Bokito from the Netherlands?*

[SFX: Tension rising, silence growing heavier.]

Dr. Danny Vendramdt (cont'd) *In 2016, Harambe the gorilla took a child into his enclosure at the Cincinnati Zoo. People were quick to argue he was being protective, but here's the thing—Harambe's strength and unpredictability made it a deadly situation. Primates don't have the same moral framework we do. What Harambe saw wasn't just a child, but something in his environment that he felt needed to be controlled. Luckily, he was shot before anything worse could happen, but the potential for violence was real. That's the key.*

Reporter: *And Bokito? That case isn't as well-known.*

Dr. Danny Vendramdt: *Bokito was a Western lowland gorilla at the Rotterdam Zoo in the Netherlands. Back in 2007, he escaped from his enclosure and attacked a woman. What's important here is that this woman had visited Bokito frequently, and some said he was 'familiar' with her. But when he broke out, he sought her out specifically and dragged her across the zoo. She survived, but only barely. Again, people think these incidents are about curiosity or even affection, but they're not. It's about dominance. Bokito saw her as something in his environment that needed to be managed—violently.*

[SFX: Soft murmur of unease in the room]

Reporter: *So you're drawing parallels between these incidents and Dahlia Rhodes' kidnapping by Sasquatch?*

Dr. Danny Vendramdt: *Exactly. It's not about sex or reproduction. A creature like Sasquatch might kidnap a human for a variety of reasons. Curiosity, dominance, maybe even seeing the person as a threat. But once you're in its territory, the rules change. You're not a person to it—you're an object, part of its environment. And how it chooses to interact with you is based on what it needs or what it perceives.*

[SFX: Silence growing, the room tense]

Reporter: *Dr. Harrison, I understand your work with chimpanzees has given you insight into this kind of behavior. You've mentioned the violent tendencies in primates when dealing with humans.*

Dr. Bryan Harrison: *Yes. This isn't something to be taken lightly. Primates, particularly the larger ones, have complex social structures, but when those structures break down, or when they perceive a challenge or intrusion, their responses can be brutal. When I heard about the Sasquatch kidnapping Dahlia, I thought of what I've seen in chimpanzees. The idea that it was purely a matter of curiosity or survival—that's too simple. Primates often act out of dominance. They'll take control of a situation or an individual simply because they can.*

[SFX: Brief pause, papers shifting, the weight of Bryan's words settling.]

Dr. Bryan Harrison (continued): *I've witnessed chimpanzees tear each other apart—not for food, but for power. For control. If Sasquatch exists, and if it took Dahlia, it may not have been for any reason we can fully understand. Maybe it was curiosity, maybe it was asserting dominance over its environment, but whatever the reason, this creature views humans as part of its world, not separate from it. In that sense, Dahlia wasn't just a victim; she was an object in a struggle for dominance.*

Reporter: *So you believe this kidnapping was less about need, and more about control?*

Dr. Bryan Harrison: *Yes. If we look at primate behavior as a model, we see that the most violent encounters often have nothing to do with food or survival. Chimps, for example, will kill out of sheer power plays. This isn't a predator hunting prey—it's an animal establishing control over its domain. And Sasquatch, assuming it follows similar social patterns, may see humans as just another part of that domain. Dahlia was unfortunate enough to get caught in it.*

Dr. Danny Vendramdt: *Spot on. Whether we like it or not, humans are intruders to these creatures. If they perceive us as a threat or even just an unknown factor, the response can be... lethal. It doesn't have to be about reproduction or survival. Sometimes, it's about power. And once that line is crossed, it's hard to know what comes next.*

Reporter: *And that's what happened with Dahlia?*

Dr. Danny Vendramdt: *Possibly. And that's what makes it so dangerous. Sasquatch, if it exists, isn't playing by our rules. It's a force in its environment, and humans are just another element to manipulate or destroy as it sees fit. It's not about malice, it's about control.*

Dr. Bryan Harrison: *And that's what makes this so terrifying. The unpredictability. This isn't a creature operating by our moral codes or social expectations. It may have kidnapped Dahlia for any number of reasons, but at the end of the day, it's about power. Just like a chimp might kill without reason, a Sasquatch might take a human to show that it can. And the outcome of that... we don't want to imagine.*

[SFX: Silence, tension in the air, the weight of their words settling in the studio.]

CHAPTER 24

The storm that had struck the Savage River State Forest had passed. But its effects remained while the rain had stopped, leaving a thick, overwhelming humidity. The atmospheric pressure mixed with the anxiety of another Sasquatch assault.

"I don't see 'em yet," Eb said, spying from their defense.

The deluge covered their bodies in moisture, making them vulnerable to trench foot and other ailments. Precipitation had coated their weapons, making them overly reliant on the primitive defense established by Accidental.

"They're here," Dirty Chap said.

The ground thundered beneath them.

"I see 'em!" Eb yelled and oriented his weapon.

A terrible creature burst from the shadow-covered forest. The Sasquatch barreled forward on all fours. Its monstrous hands and feet launched it forward in a horrible stride, utterly undeterred by the mud-covered soil.

Eb fired—*BANG BANG BANG!*

The creature moved too fast to get a decent sight.

No longer did the ape chirp with its panty-hoots, no—it let its intentions known; the monster roared—*raaaawr.*

Eb still clutched his weapon, but his whole body trembled as he watched the monster's approach. Time slowed. At that moment, Eb's eyes widened, fixed on the ape.

The team opened up again—*BANG BANG BANG BANG!*

The monster howled, and in its death spiral, it continued its forward momentum. It was too big to die immediately. Blood seeped from its body, but its heart still thudded in its chest.

It beat its chest, howling as it did—*RAAWR*—and jumped forward. The Sasquatch crashed into their defense.

Dirty Chap screamed out in agony. The beast grabbed Dirty Chap's foot.

The monster pulled Dirty Chap behind him, past the defense, as if to return its prize to its nest. Dirty Chap dragged behind the great beast. Mud coated his body. Eb and the team directed their weapons but slowed their rate of fire, fearing they would hit Dirty Chap, relying on a well-aimed headshot.

The Sasquatch swung Dirty Chap by the foot—*WHAAM!*

Dirty Chap slammed into the base of a white poplar.

"Aargh!" Dirty Chap wailed—his agony evident.

The Sasquatch swung him again—*WHAAM!*

And again—*WHAAM!*

That sound, Eb thought, *oh, that sound.*

Dirty Chap's skull cracked against the tree. The monster's eyes gleamed with evident satisfaction, and then the beast swung again—*WHAAM!*

"Fire!" Eb yelled.

Now, knowing their friend was dead, they unleashed a symphony of destruction. The rounds struck the Sasquatch's head—killing it instantly.

Eb stood frozen, the horror of the scene clawing at his soul. Dirty Chap, who had always been the loudest, the joker among them, now lay silent.

Suddenly, Eb was ripped from his mournful pause as Cora grabbed his shoulder.

"More!" she said. "More!"

And there before them, four more Sasquatch barreled forward.

"Now!" Eb's voice broke through the terror.

Accidental now had a better understanding of the creatures' timing and movements. With trembling hands, Accidental pulled the rope, unleashing their trap. The heavy, brutal log trap swung down from the canopy, crashing through the clearing. It struck the first beast, snapping bone and tearing flesh, sending the creature airborne. It slammed into the soil—with its total body weight landing on its neck. The monster's head lay perpendicular to its body—its broken neck evident.

"Move!" Doc yelled, his voice still weak from his injuries. But his cries were too late. The shadow—a new Sasquatch—launched into their defense. The beast shot its head forward, biting Doc and latching its terrible fangs onto his hand. It pulled back with Doc's hand dangling from its teeth. Its eyes, with a red baleful gleam, locked onto Doc's bones as it shook its head left to right. The crunch of bone and the tearing of flesh could be heard over Doc's scream.

Doc fell back, holding his bloody stump skyward. It was clear he was falling into shock, but he sat upright, staring at the stump with a marked curiosity. His eyes, wide and disbelieving, locked onto the place where his hand had been, his mouth opening in a silent scream that echoed only in the deepest recesses of the mind.

The Sasquatch stood back, smiling and jumping up and down in an evident display of pleasure. It shot its head forward again, this time latching its terrible fangs into Doc's foot.

The remaining team no longer feared striking their friend and unloaded munitions into the blood-coated beast.

Doc's scream filled the air.

"Doc!" Cora's voice, filled with anguish, reached Eb's ears, but she was cut off by another rock, hurled from the shadows, slamming into the tree beside her.

Doc's eyes fluttered, his breath shallow, and his body finally grew still.

The beasts, relentless and merciless, moved again. Accidental pulled the rope, releasing the second log, and it swung down, striking two more Sasquatch. Their bodies crumpled beneath the weight.

Still, more shadows moved—more creatures barreled toward them.

"C'mon!" Eb yelled. "We gotta—"

Accidental screamed, silencing Eb's command.

Eb turned, his heart in his throat. Then he saw it—the head of Accidental, severed from his body, flying through the air. Accidental's head landed with a wet thud at Eb's feet.

The Sasquatch closed in.

Eb's breath came in ragged bursts as he stumbled. Cora's panicked breaths filled his ears, her voice a distant echo in the madness. He reached for her, his fingers grabbing her arm.

"We have to go," he said.

One final beast pushed toward them. As they ran, Eb drew his pistol. The monster crashed in on them—*BANG!*

Eb fired his pistol, point-blank at the monster's skull—*BANG!*

The beast, though dead, couldn't stop its momentum. It fell forward, slamming into Eb. Eb rushed forward.

The rain. The pursuit had kept them so disoriented that they hadn't been able to find their location.

Now they stood on the bank of the Savage River. The dead body landed on Eb's leg. Cora and Eb, with the dead beast on them, slid down the muddy riverbank.

Rocks and slippery soil slid underfoot, dragging them toward the river below. The rushing water roared in their ears, and the forest screamed above.

And then they hit the water. The river swallowed them, its powerful current pulling them below.

Eerie Ebenezer Podcast, Special Guest Dr. Bryan Harrison [Continued]

Eerie Ebenezer: *Man... I gotta say, I'm almost hesitant to press you on this, Bryan. I mean, it's clear that these creatures left a real mark on you. You seem... I dunno, affected by all this in a pretty deep way.*

Dr. Bryan Harrison: [pausing] *Well, it's complicated. As a scientist, I have a responsibility to share the truth about what I've seen and studied, right? That's part of what drives progress. But as a person, as a human being, these experiences... they're... let's just say they're hard to integrate. You know? These facts aren't easy to live with.*

Eerie Ebenezer: *Yeah, I can respect that. It's that sense of duty to get the info out there, even when it's heavy, right? But, man, this part I've been meaning to ask you about—it's weird, I know, but you've mentioned encounters where great apes, especially chimps and gorillas, just... aren't even fazed by gunfire?*

Dr. Bryan Harrison: [nodding] *Yes, that's right. It's not as uncommon as you might think. And this is where things get interesting, because, if you examine their behavior under stress, especially when they feel threatened, you'll see that it aligns with their evolutionary history. Their nervous system is primed for survival, right? And firearms, well, they don't necessarily trigger that immediate retreat response we might expect.*

Eerie Ebenezer: *That's wild, man. So, you've got this story about your buddy, right? The one who was a big game hunter and an academic? You've told me about this hunt in Cameroon, led by a Baka guide, right? They run into a bunch of chimps?*

Dr. Bryan Harrison: [nodding] *Yes, exactly. My colleague—he was an experienced primatologist, very knowledgeable about great apes. But he also had a side hobby as a big game hunter, which is... an interesting combination, to say the least. They were tracking through the forests with a Baka guide, and at one point, they found themselves face-to-face with a large troop of chimpanzees. Now, in situations like that, the goal is usually to avoid confrontation. My friend, though, made the decision to fire a warning shot. He thought he could scare them off—just like with most animals.*

Eerie Ebenezer: *Yeah, man, I've seen the footage. It's up on YouTube, right? It's intense.*

Dr. Bryan Harrison: *Yes, part of it is. But what most people saw online... well, that's only half the story. They didn't see the full outcome of that encounter. And, frankly, I don't think they'd want to.*

Eerie Ebenezer: *Whoa. James, pull that up real quick.*

[The clip begins to play, and Eerie watches closely.]

Eerie Ebenezer: *Okay, here it is. So they're moving through the trees, right? You can see three—no, four chimps. And your friend fires, but... man, they're not backing down. In fact, they're speeding up. They're coming right at him.*

Dr. Bryan Harrison: [somberly] *Yes, exactly. Chimps are incredibly powerful, far stronger than humans, pound for pound. What's even more fascinating is their lack of hesitation in a moment like that. The gunshot didn't deter them in the slightest. They've evolved to be... well, to be relentless when they feel threatened or provoked. The problem here is that my colleague underestimated their resilience and their aggression.*

Eerie Ebenezer: *Man! So... what happened next?*

Dr. Bryan Harrison: [pausing] *Well... let's just say it didn't end well for either of them. My friend, and the Baka guide with him... they didn't survive. The chimps, they attacked with such intensity that... well, let's just say neither man had an open casket funeral.*

PART III

Interview with MAJ Tommy Luola, aired on WMSC Maryland News.
Audio Transcript

Reporter: *Today, we are talking with MAJ Tommy Luola, a man who served alongside Ebenezer Edwards and wants to set the record straight.*

MAJ Tommy Luola: *Thank you for having me.*

Reporter: *Now, we wanted to clarify—you reached out to us.*

MAJ Tommy Luola: *That's right.*

Reporter: *Why is that?*

MAJ Tommy Luola: *I wanted to explain Eb's actions. The way things have been reported, the truth's gotten muddied. I need people to know what actually happened.*

Reporter: *Misconstrued?*

MAJ Tommy Luola: *Exactly. Some have painted Eb as reckless, maybe even stupid. But Eb wasn't stupid. He was doing what he was trained to do, what we're all trained to do.*

Reporter: *And what's that?*

MAJ Tommy Luola: *That you never leave someone behind. Sure, you could look at it statistically, mathematically—Dahlia Rhodes? They could've left her behind. Most would've. Eb could've cut his losses and called it a day. But he didn't. He stuck it out. And that... that's the point.*

Reporter: *But why? Why keep driving his team forward when he was putting all those lives at risk—his team and Cora's—for what? Was there even evidence that Dahlia Rhodes was still alive?*

MAJ Tommy Luola: *Because he had to.*

Reporter: *Had to? Was it just duty?*

MAJ Tommy Luola: *Look, Eb was burned out. I'd seen it myself. But even after everything, that sense of duty never left him. The man believed in what we stand for—what all soldiers stand for. You can call it duty if you want. I call it being human.*

Reporter: *Duty? Some are saying the only reason Eb pushed that team was for financial gain. That he knew the*

Rhodes estate had, what appeared to be, unlimited financial resources. That Ebenezer Edwards only pushed the team because she was an heiress.

MAJ Tommy Luola: *And I'd say that before she was an heiress, she was a person. That simple fact—that she was a living, breathing person—is why Eb pushed so hard. He wasn't in it for the money. He didn't care about that. He cared because someone's life was on the line.*

Reporter: *Are you saying that Eb wasn't foolish? That he taught the world something?*

MAJ Tommy Luola: *Yes, I am. Eb showed us that no matter how tough things get, you don't stop. You keep pushing. You keep fighting. No matter what. And he taught the world that we don't leave our own behind. Ever.*

Reporter: *Some still question the decisions that cost so many lives. What do you say to them?*

MAJ Tommy Luola: *I say, go ahead and question it. You weren't there. You weren't on the ground. It's easy to sit behind a desk and pick apart the choices of a man facing death in the wild. But when you're in it, when the stakes are that high, you make the call. Eb made the right call.*

Reporter: *But you have to admit the outcome... the outcome was less than ideal.*

[There's a long pause. The tension is palpable, and the weight of the next words carries a deeper meaning than any answer so far.]

MAJ Tommy Luola: *No. It wasn't the end state anyone wanted.*

Reporter: *So what's next? Where do we go from here?*

MAJ Tommy Luola: *That's the question, isn't it?*

[The silence hangs heavy. The interview ends, but the feeling that something remains unresolved lingers in the air. The story isn't over.]

CHAPTER 1

"Cora!" Eb yelled as he stood on the bank, his eyes scanning for her through the blur of rain and darkness.

"There!" He spotted her, in a flash of movement, half-submerged, being carried downstream by the surging current. Her long black hair sprayed up from the water before she was sucked back under.

Without thinking, Eb dove back into the river, the freezing water biting into his skin. With aggressive strokes, he pushed toward her. The rain had swollen the river, increasing its flow and speed, but still—if there was any hope—Eb had to try. Adrenaline coursed through his body, giving him strength he didn't know he had left.

His hand latched onto her heel, fingers clenching around her like a lifeline. He yanked her up, pulling her close in a tight grip, keeping her head above water. They slammed into the bank, mud and water splashing around them as they crashed ashore.

"Cora!" he shouted again, panic breaking through his voice.

She coughed, sputtering as water poured from her nostrils and mouth. Her body shook, her breath ragged. Eb pulled her fully onto the shore, his own chest heaving with exhaustion, the cold settling deep in his bones. He was soaked, freezing, and aching, but it didn't matter—not now.

Cora gasped, gulping air like a drowning woman just rescued from the depths. Eb held her tight, his arms around her, pressing her close, trying to feel her heartbeat against his chest.

Her bun, once tightly wound, had come completely undone. Long strands of her black hair now hung down, feral and soaked. Even now, in the chaos they faced, he found her beautiful. Distractingly so. If a few unbound strands had been alluring—her hair now, completely feral, the long black locks hanging to her shoulders—was intoxicating.

"Thank God..." Eb muttered, his voice a raw whisper.

Cora pressed her head against his chest. Her whole body rose and fell as she fought to breathe.

"Don't let go," she said.

"Never," Eb said, tightening his grip. His teeth chattered with a violent fanaticism. The overpowering cold gnawed at him, but his focus was on her—keeping her safe, keeping her warm.

As he shifted, something felt off. The familiar weight of the Saint Jude pendant around his neck—Doc's pendant—was gone. His hand reached for the chain, but it wasn't there. The realization hit him hard. He had lost it in the river.

Finally, Cora pulled back, wiping water from her face. Her lips were blue, and her hands shook.

"We… we need to get warm," she said, her voice barely audible.

Eb nodded. "We'll freeze if we stay out here much longer."

They both knew it. The cold was creeping deeper, the risk of hypothermia growing with every second. The rain had turned everything into a swamp of mud and water, making movement difficult, but they couldn't stay by the river's edge—it was too exposed, too dangerous.

Struggling to their feet, they stumbled together, leaning on each other for balance. Their bodies were too weak, too drained to concentrate. In their weakened state, they traveled in a pattern searching for cover. They needed protection—thicket, a rock formation, anything to shield them from the elements.

The storm raged on, the trees swaying in the wind as they pushed forward. Every step was an effort, their limbs stiff from the cold, their soaked clothes weighing them down.

"Cora, we're... we're gonna be okay," Eb said, though the confidence in his voice faltered. His mind raced with thoughts of pneumonia, hypothermia—every worst-case scenario playing out in his head.

Cora nodded, but her eyes were unfocused. "If we can just... get through the night."

They kept moving, clinging to the hope of finding shelter. The rain was relentless, drumming against the trees and drowning out almost every other sound—almost.

And then Cora stopped.

"Do you hear it?" she asked, her voice sharp despite the exhaustion.

Eb stilled, holding his breath. "Do you hear it?" Cora asked again. Eb closed his eyes, allowing his ears to take in all sensory details. He relaxed his mind. He allowed his body to focus and move past the rush of the river and the ever-present tinnitus that plagued him.

A woman's scream.

"Someone's out there," Eb said, his eyes narrowing as he looked into Cora's.

The voice was distant but unmistakable.

"Help me!" the voice screamed. "Anyone, puh-lease!"

"We're still in the ballpark," Eb said, his mind racing. Despite the turmoil they had faced—despite their disorientation—their original sign-cutting had led them in the right direction.

"You hear that too?" Eb asked, ensuring he wasn't hallucinating.

Cora's eyes widened, and she nodded. "Yes," she whispered. "That voice... is my sister's."

As they pressed forward, Cora's hand instinctively went to her chest, clutching something around her neck. It was the pendant. She looked down, startled.

Eb noticed, his eyes widening. "Cora... where did you get that?"

She looked up at him, confused. "I don't know—it must have come off you in the river."

Eb reached out and took the Saint Jude pendant from her hand, his fingers lingering on the chain. It felt strange in his grip, cold and soaked, but somehow it felt heavier now. He gave her a small smile, though his exhaustion was evident.

"It looks like we're not done with this thing either," he said.

Cora nodded, her eyes meeting his with understanding. Eb slid the pendant back around his neck.

This lost cause wasn't over—not yet.

CHAPTER 2

Eb shivered. Eb and Cora held hands, helping each other along as they pushed through the mud-soaked bank and onto the riverbank shore of the Savage River. Cora wrapped her arms around him as they stood on the bank. And pressing her head into his chest, she sobbed.

"We're going to be alright," Eb said, patting her back.

Deep down inside, he felt as though he was lying. But what was he supposed to say? This situation was unprecedented.

Dahlia had cried out for them—their mission wasn't over. Human life had to be protected.

But their lives—their humanity had been forever scarred by the carnage they'd witnessed. They had just seen Doc's head viciously ripped from his body. They had thrown Doc's head just as they had thrown rocks—just as they had thrown feces—as a threat. There was no care, no regard for Doc.

Eb's hands involuntarily balled into fists.

"We're going to get 'em," Eb said, patting her back, "we'll get 'em yet."

And it was that—not the comfort, but the promise of revenge in the immediate face of tragedy that seemed to console Cora.

She lifted her head from his chest, nodding, "Ok."

"Let's see what you got in the inventory," Eb said.

"That thing almost drowned me," she said.

"In the end," Eb said, "you'll be glad you had it."

Cora slid the assault pack off her back and sat it in the moist grass. Eb knelt down and unzipped the bag.

"Now, what are we looking at?" Cora said, her face scrunched like a prune as she peered into the assault pack.

"You were carrying our less lethal bag," Eb said. "When you volunteered to carry something—we figured we could give you this."

"So, is this like the throw away bag?" Cora said. "You guys just gave this to me to let me feel like I was part of the team?"

"Hey," Eb said. "You told us you wanted to carry something—you insisted."

Cora stared inside the bag.

"So this bag is useless?" she asked. She reached inside and pulled out a tube-shaped device. "What are we going to do with this?"

"That's a collapsible baton," Eb said. With practiced proficiency, he extended his arm. The baton didn't extend all the way, instead only revealing half.

"And it's rusted?" Cora asked.

"That's why we always brought this," he said, and reaching in, he pulled out a blue and yellow can.

"WD-40?"

"Let's just say, the Rodney King incident really hurt the sell of these things," Eb said. "The optics of them aren't great. They're decent tools, but we didn't keep them on us."

Cora pulled out another first item. It was a canister with faded paper crudely clinging to it.

"How old is this thing?" Cora asked and handed it to him.

"You really did a number picking us, didn't you?" Eb smirked. "Dark Waters recalled this. It's an old-school bottle of OC spray."

"Great," Cora said, "So it's no good."

"Oh, I beg to differ, sweetheart," Eb said. "This cannister didn't get recalled because it was no good—"

"Then why did it get recalled?"

Eb smiled wide, exposing his teeth. "Because it was alcohol based."

"So it's still outdated," Cora said, shaking her head.

"C'mon, now," Eb said. "Didn't you do more in college than just play softball... didn't you just hear what I said?"

Eb accepted it but barely looked at the canister. His fingers traced the label absentmindedly. In hindsight, something more straightforward and primal should've been their first line of defense. The creatures didn't register the gunfire, not how humans would. But they might've recognized tools—clubs, chemical clouds—those.

"In hindsight," Eb said, feeling a lump growing in his throat, "this is the stuff we should have used first."

Our friends might still be here, he thought.

He felt Cora's powerful gaze falling on him. He shook his head slightly, not wanting to explain the full depth of his thoughts just yet. They didn't have time for second guesses. She continued sorting through the bag, pulling out another canister.

"Tear gas?" Cora said. "So they'll stop their protests?"

Cora shook her head, her frustration evident.

"Hey," Eb reached out and touched her face. "Trust me, I have a plan."

She pulled out the smoke grenade next and placed it on the ground with the others. "Smoke 'em out?"

Eb turned away from Cora. He studied the mouth of the nest, where they had heard the cries.

"Yeah," Eb said. "Something like that."

Interview with MAJ Tommy Luola, aired on WMSC Maryland News
Audio Transcript

Reporter: *Earlier, you mentioned Eb's idealism, but, Major, let's be honest, reports from the field described him as... well, a grouch.*

MAJ Tommy Luola: [calmly] *I'd call that part of his evolution, his personal arc. We all grow in combat situations—his growth was evident in his actions. The reports make that clear.*

Reporter: *Hmm. But you refer to his prudence as though it were a defining trait. How can you justify that? In the end, we're talking about someone who led an assault with batons and OC spray, of all things.*

MAJ Tommy Luola: [measured tone] *Yes. And I'd remind you of something Lt. General Harold G. Moore once said: "Three strikes and you are not out." In warfare, there's always more you can do—always another tactic, another opportunity to exploit.*

Reporter: [with a slight scoff] *That's an inspiring quote, but Major, they'd already failed. They had military-grade weapons, and they still couldn't get the job done. Guns weren't enough, and now we're supposed to believe they thought batons would be?*

MAJ Tommy Luola: [steady] *They hadn't failed. What they did was learn. Warfare isn't static, and their approach evolved. They understood that these creatures weren't enemies in the conventional sense. They were facing something entirely different—let's call it what it was: an animalistic adversary.*

Reporter: [incredulous] *An adversary that soundly beat them, Major. If guns and traps didn't work, how on earth did they expect batons and pepper spray to succeed?*

MAJ Tommy Luola: [patient, with a touch of gravitas] *They analyzed the terrain, assessed their enemy's behavior, and adapted accordingly. You see, if you point a firearm at a gorilla, it doesn't perceive it as a threat. The Australian Army, as you might recall, was humbled by emus. These were the lessons Eb and Cora internalized. They knew they needed a different approach, and that's what they used.*

Reporter: [with a sneer] *You're suggesting that a soldier—your soldier—*

MAJ Tommy Luola: *Paratrooper—*

Reporter: [coughs] *Paratrooper—charged into a nest of what you've called "animalistic adversaries" armed with nothing but a collapsible baton and a Bowie knife? That's the strategy you respect?*

MAJ Tommy Luola: [with a thin smile, unruffled] *Respect is earned through intelligent decision-making. And no, they didn't walk in empty-handed. You're missing a critical component of the plan.*

Reporter: [mocking] *Really? Because my research shows that those were the tools they carried. What am I missing, Major?*

MAJ Tommy Luola: [leaning forward slightly, with quiet authority] *The special ingredient.*

CHAPTER 3

Eb moved through the thick underbrush. They now walked back toward the river bank, returning to where they had started. They had stepped away and rehearsed their plan, ensuring it was no longer a deliberate thought but a simple action.

"I haven't practiced that much since softball," Cora said from behind.

Eb smiled slightly but didn't break stride. He knew she was trying to inject a bit of normalcy into their situation. Though he appreciated it, his mind remained fixed on what lay ahead.

"It wasn't practice," he replied. "It was rehearsal. We've got to get this right."

They had spent hours preparing and reviewing each step, movement, and possibility. It was no longer about just surviving—it was about executing the plan.

In his left hand, he gripped the baton, wrapped tightly in the remnants of his torn shirt, soaked in oil. In his right hand, the Kukri blade felt solid and reliable. Behind him, Cora followed closely, her Glock held in the low-ready position. He could hear her steady steps and her breath as she scanned the dense forest. The torn fabric of her shirt revealed the patches of her vitiligo-marked skin, but he didn't dwell on it. There wasn't time for distraction.

He had reconnoitered the river earlier, searching for a shallow path where they could cross without being swept away. They had marked the way with a strip torn from Cora's shirt. The path was just ahead now.

"There it is," Eb said. "It's time."

The dark and swift river came into view, the water cold against their legs as they waded in. Eb kept his grip on the baton firm, his focus sharp. He felt the icy current pull at his legs as they pushed through. The crossing was quick, their movements practiced and deliberate. They reached the other side, dripping but determined. Ahead, the hut stood in the clearing formed in the muddy river bank.

But despite the peril they faced, Eb found strength. From behind, he could sense a renewed energy in Cora as she walked. He felt how she moved, and her steps quickened slightly as they neared the hut. His own breath steadied; every muscle coiled with anticipation.

Without warning, Cora came up beside him and pressed a quick kiss to his lips. It startled him, unexpected and sudden.

"For good luck," she said softly, her breath warm against his skin.

Eb blinked, taken aback for just a moment. "Thanks," he muttered, his eyes shifting away before refocusing on the task. "We're going to need it."

They moved forward, the world around them eerily silent. They were moving to the structures Heinrich Aristov had purchased—the mock-rock enclosures. With each step, the cave grew closer, the shadows deepening. As they reached the entrance, Eb stopped. His eyes locked onto the darkness inside. His grip tightened on the baton, the oil-soaked cloth wrapped tightly around it, ready.

Cora stood beside him, close but silent. Eb could hear the rustle of fabric as she reached into her pocket. The slight sound of the lighter flicking open broke the stillness, and a small flame danced to life.

"Come on," she said, her voice low, calm, controlled. "The final touch."

Eb didn't take his eyes off the threat ahead. His heart beat steadily in his chest—muscles taut.

"Yes," he said quietly, lifting the baton and holding it out. The flame from Cora's lighter touched the oil-soaked rag, and the fire took quickly, spreading along the length of the baton.

"Here goes nothing," Cora said.

The flames licked up, casting twisted shadows that seemed to writhe and pulse. They knew the peril that awaited them in that black pit. Death awaited them in that terrible abyss. The air was heavy, thick with the promise of an ancient malevolent force.

Every step had been rehearsed, every detail pondered in dark hours, but now, as they stood on the threshold of that dreadful place, all preparation seemed a vain attempt to stave off the inevitable.

But despite this—despite the crushing anxiety of the inevitable—they did not stop.

Muscles tensed. Weapons ready. The path was set. They stood at the threshold. Their eyes locked upon the void before them. They felt the fear, thick and cold.

Together, they stepped forward. The darkness swallowed them, thick and suffocating. Their hearts pounded. But their resolve was solid—their will unbroken. They knew they might not come back. Still, they pressed on. Not out of hope. Not for glory. But because this was their fight.

The cave loomed. The unknown waited. And they crossed into the darkness and in defiance of the horrors that awaited, they dared to hope.

Eerie Ebenezer Paranormal Podcast
Special Guest: Danny Vendramdt, Author of Them Against Us: How We Defeated The Neanderthals

(Interview, continued)

Eb: *Mate, your book—Them Against Us—it's like throwing a grenade into the middle of the scientific community. People are either loving it or losing their minds over it.*

Danny: [chuckles] *Yeah, well, that's what happens when you stop sugar-coating things, right? Too many folks out there want to paint this romantic picture of Neanderthals as misunderstood cousins. I'm not here for that. I'm here to talk about the real world—about how we survived. It wasn't pretty.*

Eb: *Yeah, I got that loud and clear. You don't buy the whole "peaceful coexistence" theory at all. You've gone all in on this idea that it was us or them. No middle ground.*

Danny: *Right, because that's what the evidence shows. We weren't making friends with them; we were fighting to survive. Neanderthals were apex predators, stronger and faster than us. We didn't win by luck, and it wasn't just intelligence that gave us the edge. The real difference between us and them? It was fire, mate.*

Eb: *Fire?*

Danny: *Yep. But before I get to that, let me ask you something. What's the weakness of every monster in folklore? Think about it—Dracula, Frankenstein's monster, any of those classic horrors. What takes them down?*

Eb: *I don't know... silver bullets? Stakes? Sunlight? Is this some kind of metaphor?*

Danny: [laughs] *Nah, bloke. It's not a metaphor. It's* pseudo-memory. *It's deep in our psyche. Fire. They're all vulnerable to fire. The orange rose, as I like to call it. That's what really separates us from beasts. Neanderthals didn't have the same mastery of fire. Maybe they could sit around one that was started by a lightning strike or something, but they didn't* own *it like we did.*

Eb: *So they didn't use fire like we did?*

Danny: *Well, they've found ashes at some Neanderthal sites, places like Pech de l'Azé in France or La Chapelle-aux-Saints. Yeah, they had fire around. But there's no definitive proof they could make it. No flint-and-steel tools, no clear evidence of consistent fire production. Even in mainstream circles, the debate is still going. Did Neanderthals* master *fire, or were they just opportunistic users? Did they sit by it when it was there but go without when it wasn't?*

Eb: *So you're saying they might've just kept it going when they had it, but they couldn't start it themselves?*

Danny: *Exactly. And that's a huge difference, mate. Being able to start fire when you need it—that's power. That's control. Neanderthals might have had fire when the opportunity struck, but we* owned *it. We could make it anywhere, anytime. That's why we survived and they didn't. It wasn't just a matter of strength or intelligence. Fire gave us a weapon they couldn't match.*

Eb: *And mainstream science still hasn't settled on this? Whether they mastered fire or not?*

Danny: *Nah, the debate's still going strong. Some scientists say Neanderthals knew how to manage fire, others argue they were just opportunists who used it when it was there. But here's the thing—what does your gut tell you? What does our pseudo-memory say? Look at the stories we've been telling for centuries. Monsters, beasts, they all fall to fire. Deep down, we know it's not just a tool. It's survival. It's domination of the environment.*

Eb: *So, fire wasn't just about cooking or warmth—it was control?*

Danny: *That's it, mate. Fire was* everything. *It wasn't just about getting through the night; it was about reshaping the world. Neanderthals didn't have that level of control. We used fire to drive away predators, to open up new lands, to give ourselves more energy through cooked food. It let us push into places they couldn't go. It scared them, just like it does with all beasts.*

Eb: *So fire was the great equalizer?*

Danny: *More than that, mate—it was the great advantage. Without it, we wouldn't be having this conversation. And deep down, I think we all know that. Fire wasn't just warmth and safety—it was power. It was how we won. That's why every monster in every old story fears it. Because we do too. Somewhere in our heads, we remember how we used fire to keep the darkness at bay. We mastered it, and Neanderthals couldn't. And that's the difference between us and them.*

Eb: *Man, that's deep. So fire's not just survival—it's in our DNA, our stories, our history.*

Danny: *Exactly, mate. It's why we're still here. We didn't just adapt—we* dominated. *We wielded fire not just as a tool...we used it as a weapon.*

CHAPTER 4

Eb, with Cora following behind, stepped into the darkness. The makeshift torch illuminated the cave, casting flickering shadows against the jagged stone walls. Fueled by the soaked rag, the flame crackled and hissed as it struggled to push back the overwhelming gloom. The stench of the cave hit Eb with an instinctive revulsion that rippled through his body. Cora moved close behind him, her breath shallow but steady, Glock in one hand, WD-40 clutched tightly in the other.

Eb waved the burning baton ahead, trying to push through the dark. The cavern was vast—shadows deeper than they'd expected. For a moment, it felt as though the cave itself was alive, breathing in the flame and spitting it back in erratic bursts. Then, out of the corner of his eye, Eb spotted a figure huddled in the shadows—small, unmoving.

Dahlia.

Her body slumped against the far wall, her hair wild and matted. Even in the low light, he could see the exhaustion in her face, the way her breathing struggled to catch. She was alive. That brief flicker of relief hit, but it quickly gave way to something colder, sharper. Because Dahlia wasn't alone.

The Alpha.

The massive silhouette loomed at the far end of the cave—a grotesque, hulking figure that dwarfed the darkness around it. A broad, distended belly hung over thick, muscular legs, and its eyes—those horrible, glowing red eyes—tracked their every move. The creature's face twisted into something unnatural, a grin. Its breath came out in slow, rasping grunts, thick with animalistic malice.

Eb's heart pounded with a hammer-like intensity. Blood roared in his ears as the primal fury of the moment consumed him.

"There's the Alpha," Cora whispered.

The Alpha's grin widened. Slowly, it raised a massive, clawed hand and pointed at them with deliberate cruelty. Its yellowed teeth gleamed in the firelight as a high-pitched, guttural squeal tore from its throat. It wasn't just a noise—it was an order.

Eb's eyes darted to Dahlia. Her wrists were shackled to the wall, her arms barely moving, fear etched on her face. There was no way she was getting out without help. He glanced at Cora, his jaw set.

"Stay on track," he muttered. "We finish this."

Then the Alpha's command was answered.

A smaller, wiry Sasquatch lunged out of the shadows, its eyes wild, its nostrils flaring. It moved fast—too fast—but Eb was already in motion.

WHOOSH!

Eb swung the burning baton wide, fire arcing through the air and illuminating the cave in a sudden, blinding flash. The flames caught the smaller creature's attention just long enough.

The Sasquatch sucked in a deep breath, and that was its mistake.

The fire shot directly into the creature's exposed nostrils. Its chest expanded for a split second, and then the thing froze. There was no scream, no thrashing—just a sudden, violent stillness. The fire roared through its body from the inside, and it instantly dropped. The monster's limbs convulsed before falling silent. The cave echoed with the sound of its collapse—a dull thud followed by the sickening sizzle.

They were animals—flesh, bone, and instincts. Exposed nostrils. Unprotected. Unlike humans.

Another screech tore through the smoke-filled air.

Cora's Glock barked—*BANG*—a clean shot straight into another Sasquatch as it charged from the shadows. Its momentum didn't falter. She was ready, though, moving fast as she hurled a smoke canister toward the Alpha, gas billowing up around them, shrouding the monster in thick clouds.

Though partially obscured, the Alpha remained unmoving—its red eyes cutting through the haze.

Another creature sprang forward, larger and more aggressive than the last.

WHOOSH!

Eb swung his burning rod. The flame-wreathed baton licked the edges of the cave. The flames cast wild shadows against the walls and in the partial illumination, Eb could see the approaching beasts. The wild, glassy look of their eyes made their fear evident—but behind them stood the great Alpha—beating his chest—pressing them forward.

Another Sasquatch closed the distance. The great ape reached out with its malignant claws.

Instantly, Cora responded. She sprayed the WD-40 into the flame—*WHOOSH!* Fire leapt upon the charging beast. The orange flames danced across the fur, overwhelming the monster in pain. Its epidermis popped and sizzled.

Despite the pain he inflicted, Eb felt a pang of sympathy—but not enough to let the mission be deterred—he swung the Kukri blade—*SLASH*—penetrating the creature's hide. It stumbled forward, blinded by the fire.

"Now!" Eb said.

Instantly, Cora leaned forward, Glock extended—*BANG*—a clear shot through the ape's skull.

The Sasquatch stopped—but the flames continued.

Another, faster, stronger ape bounded toward them.

Cora fired twice—*BANG! BANG!* The bullets slowed the monster, but it didn't stop. Eb charged forward, his baton held high, the fire flickering dangerously. He brought it down—*WHOOSH*—flames leapt onto the creature's body, the fur igniting instantly. Then the blade—*SLASH*—cleaved through its neck. The body dropped.

The cave reverberated with a symphony of madness—a macabre sonata of flickering flames entwined with the ghastly wails of the dying.

Smoke, fire, and the stench of burning fur filled the space. The dying creatures' wails echoed off the walls in a terrible chorus. But still, the Alpha stood. His countenance bespoke bitter anguish, combined with disdain and malignity, while its unearthly ugliness rendered it almost too horrible for human eyes.

The Alpha, evidently noticing it, drew back. With a grim sort of smile—which showed more than he had yet done his protuberant teeth—the black lips fell back over them—opening like evil flower petals. The ape bared its teeth—sharp and pointed. Its scarlet eyes gleamed in triumph at Eb's fear. The monster smiled, giving a horrible baleful gleam that would make even Judas Iscariot in Hell shudder.

The firelight reflected off Cora's face as she threw another smoke canister. A cloud of gas swirled thick around the Alpha.

Eb stood in front of Cora, just as they'd rehearsed. In defiance of the monster, he held high his flame-wreathed baton and readied the Kukri blade with lethal intent.

"Now," he said. "We move to the final boss."

Interview with MAJ Tommy Luola, aired on WMSC Maryland News
Audio Transcript

Reporter: *So…the secret ingredient, it was fire?*

MAJ Tommy Luola: *I would say it was…a fire…a particular fire.*

Reporter: *Now... correct me if I'm wrong, but it seems like Eb was taking a step backward in terms of modern technology, wasn't he?*

MAJ Tommy Luola: [smirking] *You could say that. But in warfare, we sometimes call that getting back to basics—fundamentals like fire and steel. Sometimes, the oldest tools are the best tools.*

Reporter: *Hmm, basics? That sounds a bit... barbaric, doesn't it?*

MAJ Tommy Luola: [chuckling] *War itself is barbaric, ma'am. But sometimes you've got to step back from all the tech and see the truth: peace is found when you understand the value of life. That's what Eb figured out.*

Reporter: *So you're saying he went primitive to find peace?*

MAJ Tommy Luola: [nodding] *Exactly. There's an old saying—'the fire that warms also burns.' In that cave, it wasn't just about the less-lethal gear, no. It was something deeper. That fire he lit wasn't just to fight the enemy, it was to save a life.*

Reporter: *Yes, you're talking about Dahlia, right?*

MAJ Tommy Luola: [leaning forward] *Yes, but not just her. I'm talking about the fire inside him. There, in that dark, damp place, surrounded by death and danger, he wasn't just fighting monsters. He was protecting life—his own, Dahlia's, Cora's. With her at his back, he realized what it meant to serve, to defend. He learned that life—human life—was sacred.*

Reporter: *Sacred, you say?*

MAJ Tommy Luola: [softly] *Eb knew his mission wasn't just to fight. It was to protect. To be a guardian, a sheepdog standing between the wolves and the flock. In that moment, despite the fear, despite the odds, he understood that even in the darkest corners, where evil lurks, hope can bloom. His hope—it burned bright. And in the presence of evil, he stood there with his fire, and in that flame, you could see defiance—you could see hope.*

CHAPTER 5

The cave pulsed with the light of dying flames. Eb waved his fire-fueled baton.
The Alpha stood and beat its chest in a gorilla-like manner. Its roar echoed against the walls.
Eb moved his knife-hand higher, giving Cora a better sight picture. Behind him, she aimed her Glock. The Austrian pistol rang out—*BANG BANG!*

The Alpha—with a speed that defied its mass—shifted laterally. Simultaneously, the Alpha struck.
The Alpha hurled a rock. The object slammed into Eb's chest—*THUD!*
He slammed to the ground—the hard surface knocking the wind from his lungs.

BANG! BANG!

Cora's pistol barked, the sound piercing the cave's smoky air. But the Alpha dodged each shot, its massive form moving with terrifying speed. Blood dripped from Eb's mouth as he forced himself back to his feet, ignoring the pain.

"Cora, reload," Eb coughed out. With pain-filled movement, he stumbled to his knees. He stepped forward, baton in hand, the flames lighting up the cave as he swung—*WHOOSH*—pushing the creature back.

The Alpha hacked and coughed, circling them, its breath labored. But it wasn't finished. It charged again, claws out, eyes locked on Cora. *BANG!* A shot hit its shoulder, another to its chest, but the beast continued its onslaught.

Eb ducked, slicing the Alpha's side—*SLASH*—blood sprayed across the stone floor. The Alpha howled. Cora fired again—*BANG*—her bullets barely slowing the monster as it lunged.
Finally, Eb swung the burning baton again—*WHOOSH*—flames caught the Alpha's fur, igniting it.
The monster danced madly—swinging its arms in wild gesticulation. The fire now consumed its whole body, from its

head down to its massive feet. But despite its pain—despite its inevitable doom—the monster continued moving.

Eb moved in, slashing with the Kukri blade—one strike, two strikes, three—all directed at its torso.

Cora stepped from behind Eb, now standing beside him. She unleashed the entire magazine—all directed at the monster's exposed, unraveling intestines.

Eb seized the moment. He stepped forward, ramming the flaming baton straight into the Alpha's exposed nostrils. The creature's eyes danced in shock. Its horrible hands clutched the baton. Vainly, it tried to pull the baton free. With an adrenaline-fueled energy, Eb pushed the baton deeper.

The burning Alpha's body trembled—teetering on its failing body. Then, with a final gasp, it fell forward. It slammed face-first onto the unforgiving soil. The flaming baton shot through the back of its skull.

"It's finished," Eb said and tossed his Kukri knife to the ground.

His ears rang with the hum of the gunfire and monster pant-hoots. Eb took a knee, trying to catch his breath. And as he did, he watched as Cora stepped forward. Bending over, she picked up the Kukri knife.

"Damn you," she whispered through her tears, her voice breaking.

"Cora," Eb said, his voice weak with fatigue.

But she didn't stop. She stepped to the monster, raised the blade, and with a hammer fist-like strike, drove the knife into the dead Alpha's skull. Again and again, she stabbed, her screams bouncing off the cave walls. Each strike opened a door to a memory—images of horror that Eb wanted to forget.

Muleskinner, screaming as the Sasquatch stomped on him. The sickening crunch of his bones beneath its massive foot. *We couldn't save him.*

Dirty Chap, lifted like a ragdoll, slammed against a tree—again and again. Blood sprayed from his mouth with each sickening impact until there was nothing left but a broken body. *We couldn't stop it.*

Doc, his eyes wide with terror, his hand and foot ripped off like toys, the Sasquatch squealing in delight, playing with its prey. *Too late to help.*

Accidental, his head ripped from his body, the Sasquatch tossing it through the air. The head smacked into the ground at Eb's feet, his lifeless eyes staring up at him. *We should've done more.*

"Cora!" Eb shouted, his voice raw with pain, both physical and emotional. But she didn't hear him, lost in her rage, her grief fueling every savage plunge of the knife.

The past weighed down on him, pressing into his chest, making it hard to breathe. He could see their faces, hear their screams, feel the helplessness all over again. His pulse quickened. His mind was flooded with horrible images—the final moments of his friends. It felt as if he was there again—back in those places of death.

"CORA!" he yelled again, louder this time, forcing the word through the suffocating weight of his memories.

She looked up from her act—her eyes swollen with grief. The knife slipped from her trembling hand. She hobbled to him. He rushed to her and wrapped his arms around her. She accepted his embrace and collapsed against him. He put his hand in her long, unbound black hair. Her sobs muffled by his chest. Eb wrapped her in a tight embrace, holding her as the weight of the battle finally sank in.

"You saved me," he said, drawing her closer and softly kissing her lips. "Now, I save you." Tears streamed down her face, and she nodded in acknowledgement.

"C'mon, Cora," Eb said. "Let's get your sister, and go home."

Cryptid Novels!

Edward J. McFadden III

THE CRYPTID CLUB

When cryptozoologist Ash Cohn receives a gold embossed printed invitation inviting him to join The Cryptid Club, he sees the resolution to all his problems.Famous cryptid scientist and biologist, Lester Treemont, one of the world's richest men, and the leader of the Cryptid Club, is dying. What he offers via his invitation is a chance to succeed him. To take over his wealth, laboratory, and discoveries. All Ash has to do is beat eight others like him in a series of tests both mental and physical involving Treemont's collection of cryptids. Seems simple enough, and Ash has nothing to lose.Nine strangers from across the globe, all with reasons for wanting to win. When they start dying one by one, the competition shifts to one of survival. Who among them will rise to the top and reign over The Cryptid Club?

William Meikle

INFESTATION

It was supposed to be a simple mission. A suspected Russian spy boat is in trouble in Canadian waters. Investigate and report are the orders. But when Captain John Banks and his squad arrive, it is to find an empty vessel, and a scene of bloody mayhem. Soon they are in a fight for their lives, for there are things in the icy seas off Baffin Island, scuttling, hungry things with a taste for human flesh. They are swarming. And they are growing. "Scotland's best Horror writer" - Ginger Nuts of Horror "The premier storyteller of our time." - Famous Monsters of Filmland

Check out other great

Cryptid Novels!

Hunter Shea

THE DOVER DEMON

The Dover Demon is real...and it has returned. In 1977, Sam Brogna and his friends came upon a terrifying, alien creature on a deserted country road. What they witnessed was so bizarre, so chilling, they swore their silence. But their lives were changed forever. Decades later, the town of Dover has been hit by a massive blizzard. Sam's son, Nicky, is drawn to search for the infamous cryptid, only to disappear into the bowels of a secret underground lair. The Dover Demon is far deadlier than anyone could have believed. And there are many of them. Can Sam and his reunited friends rescue Nicky and battle a race of creatures so powerful, so sinister, that history itself has been shaped by their secretive presence? "THE DOVER DEMON is Shea's most delightful and insidiously terrifying monster yet." – Shotgun Logic Reviews "An excellent horror novel and a strong standout in the UFO and cryptid subgenres." –Hellnotes "Non-stop action awaits those brave enough to dive into the small town of Dover, and if you're lucky, you won't see the Demon himself!" – The Scary Reviews PRAISE FOR SWAMP MONSTER MASSACRE "B-horror movie fans rejoice, Hunter Shea is here to bring you the ultimate tale of terror!" – Horror Novel Reviews "A nonstop thrill ride! I couldn't put this book down." – Cedar Hollow Horror Reviews

Armand Rosamilia

THE BEAST

The end of summer, 1986. With only a few days left until the new school year, twins Jeremy and Jack Schaffer are on very different paths. Jeremy is the geek, playing Dungeons & Dragons with friends Kathleen and Randy, while Jack is the jock, getting into trouble with his buddies. And then everything changes when neighbor Mister Higgins is killed by a wild animal in his yard. Was it a bear? There's something big lurking in the woods behind their New Jersey home.Will the police be able to solve the murder before more Middletown residents are ripped apart?

www.ingramcontent.com/pod-product-compliance
Lightning Source LLC
Chambersburg PA
CBHW061240170626
46809CB00007B/2754
* 9 7 8 1 9 2 3 1 6 5 4 0 3 *